The Queen of Put-Down

NANCY J. HOPPER

Aladdin Books
Macmillan Publishing Company
New York
Maxwell Macmillan Canada
Toronto
Maxwell Macmillan International
New York   Oxford   Singapore   Sydney

To Carolyn Frank,
who asked me to write about friendship

First Aladdin Books edition 1993
Copyright © 1991 Nancy J. Hopper

Aladdin Books   Maxwell Macmillan Canada, Inc.
Macmillan Publishing Company   1200 Eglinton Avenue East
866 Third Avenue   Suite 200
New York, NY 10022   Don Mills, Ontario M3C 3N1

Macmillan Publishing Company is part of the
Maxwell Communication Group of Companies.
Printed in the United States of America
10 9 8 7 6 5 4 3 2 1
A hardcover edition of *The Queen of Put-Down* is available from
Four Winds Press, Macmillan Publishing Company.

Library of Congress Cataloging-in-Publication Data
Hopper, Nancy J.
The queen of put-down / Nancy J. Hopper. —1st Aladdin Books ed.
p.   cm.
Summary: When she tries to befriend Sabrina, the new girl in class,
fifth-grader Cassie finds unexpected obstacles in her path, not the
least of which is Sabrina's prickly personality.
ISBN 0-689-71670-2
[1. Friendship—Fiction. 2. Behavior—Fiction. 3. Schools—
Fiction.] I. Title.
PZ7.H7792Qu 1993
[Fic]—dc20   92-19559

1

The day Sabrina Evans came to my school was hot, more like July than May. A big fly buzzed lazily outside the open windows of Room 12. We'd just returned from lunch, and I was half asleep, dreaming about my birthday, which was less than ten hours away.

Mrs. Rudolph was reviewing the metric system. As she turned to write on the board, Julius Palmenter twisted in his seat. He glared at Rob Ray, who sits behind him. Then, holding his pencil like a knife, Julius lashed out at Rob's leg.

Rob jerked away, but not fast enough. The pencil grazed his pants, leaving a long, black mark.

"He wrecked my pants!" yelled Rob, sticking his leg up in the air so everybody could see the black mark. The orange and brown pencil flashed as Julius tried to stab him again.

"Julius!" Mrs. Rudolph dropped the chalk and rushed to grab him.

Whenever Julius is in trouble, he always tries

1

to blame someone else. "Rob called me a name!" he protested.

"I did not!" said Rob.

Mrs. Rudolph wrestled the pencil from Julius and stepped back toward her desk, frowning.

"That's *my* pencil," said Julius. "You had no right to take it!"

Mrs. Rudolph took a deep breath. "You were using it to hurt Rob," she pointed out.

"I want my pencil!" Julius shouted. "Peach Fuzz gave it to me!"

That was when the rap came on our classroom door. Mrs. Rudolph looked at Julius for a moment. Then she said, "If you can control yourself the rest of the afternoon, we will discuss your pencil after school." She dropped the pencil into the top drawer of her desk, picked up the chalk from the floor, and went to the door.

After a few words with whoever was outside, Mrs. Rudolph went into the hall, leaving the door ajar behind her.

Immediately, Emily Harris, who is my best friend, leaned across the aisle toward me. "I can't wait until after school when I get my puppy," she whispered.

"I wish I could have a dog," I whispered back. "If Alfie didn't have stupid old asthma, I'd have lots of pets."

"Louie can be half yours," said Emily. Louie was the name she'd picked for her puppy.

"Thanks!" was all I had time to say because

Mrs. Rudolph had come back into the room. A new student was with her.

"Class, I'd like you to meet Sabrina Evans, who is transferring to our school from Florida," said Mrs. Rudolph. She smiled at the new girl. "Would you like to say something?"

"Hello." Sabrina's lips parted in a brief smile, revealing braces. She had a pretty oval face framed by long, curly black hair, and she was tall—even taller than Erin O'Connor, who until then had been the tallest kid in the fifth grade. Sabrina was wearing a pair of new jeans, a red belt, and a red-and-blue-plaid shirt with a ruffle down the front. She carried a blue backpack, which she kept shifting from hand to hand.

"Who wants to be Sabrina's sponsor," asked Mrs. Rudolph, "to help her feel at home and to meet new friends?"

I shot upright in my seat, waving wildly to attract Mrs. Rudolph's attention.

"Cassie," said Mrs. Rudolph, "I like your enthusiasm."

"Besides, the only empty desk is in front of her," pointed out Marietta Kirksey.

When the kids stopped laughing, Mrs. Rudolph added, "I need a few minutes to talk with Sabrina and issue her textbooks. While we're doing that, I want the rest of you to write welcome notes. Use your best handwriting, and be certain to tell Sabrina why you are glad she's here at Oakway Elementary."

3

"Dear Sabrina," I wrote, "I'm glad you came to our school because I want to be your friend." I stared at the paper for a while, then glanced across the aisle at Emily. She was bent over her desk, the tip of her tongue protruding between her lips as she wrote.

Emily and I have been best friends since the first grade. We like the same food, the same movies, and the same people. She's the perfect friend for me—except that every summer she goes to Michigan with her family. I'm left without anyone to do things with. All the other girls my age are busy with their best friends, live too far from me, or go to camp. I'm stuck hanging around the house or going places with my little brother.

Summer's a bummer.

Not this summer, I told myself as I looked at the new girl, who was turning the pages of a science workbook. Sabrina probably had trouble with math like me and hated stuck-up people. She might even have a bratty little brother.

"We can ride our bicycles out the Iron Horse Trail," I added to the sentence I'd already written in my welcome note. "You can sleep over at my house, and we'll go on hikes and swimming together."

"You have one more minute to finish your notes," Mrs. Rudolph announced. Then she told Sabrina, "I'll take a quick look at them before I hand them on to you."

During recess, which fourth and fifth grades have only in the afternoon, the boys hang around the track in groups or play baseball. Some of the girls from our room go over to the swing set, and Erin practices shooting baskets in preparation for her career as a big-time hoop star. As Emily, Marietta, Margo, and I talk together under a big oak tree near the basketball court, the sound of Erin's ball on the macadam seems part of our conversation.

That afternoon Sabrina was with us. I leaned against the tree next to Marietta, watching Erin as she practiced. She has long, skinny arms. Her legs are skinny, too, and end in huge feet. Erin's not exactly pretty, but she has beautiful hair, thick and shiny, the color of chestnuts.

"Where did you live in Florida?" Emily asked Sabrina.

"Near Disney World. My father worked there."

"Lucky!" said Marietta. "I bet you went to Disney World lots."

Sabrina shrugged. "I had a pass so I could go whenever I wanted. It got boring after a while."

I glanced at Emily. It was hard to believe Disney World could ever be boring. I wouldn't know for certain, because I've never been there, but Emily's gone twice.

"Where do you live now?" I asked.

"Outside town," Sabrina answered.

I was going to ask what street when Marietta

said, "There are six people in my family. How many in yours?"

"Three," said Sabrina. "My father, my mother, and me."

"That's like me," Emily told her.

Sabrina's cool green eyes ran over Emily's frizzy halo of yellow hair, the splotch of freckles across her nose, and her pudgy figure. It was clear that Sabrina couldn't imagine she and Emily were alike in any way.

"I'm getting a puppy after school today," Emily added. "He's a golden retriever named Louie. My mother and I are going to pick him up at the kennel."

"I have a brother named Alfie," I said. "I'd trade him for a golden retriever anytime."

Sabrina laughed along with Emily and Marietta. Margo, who is sort of awkward and bony, only smiled. She was fingering a large zit on her chin while she listened to us. "I don't have any pets," she said. "I'm allergic to cats and dogs."

Erin tried a long shot at the hoop and missed. She ran forward, caught the ball on the rebound, dribbled twice, and shot again. *Smack, smack, sprong, swish* went the basketball, going through the net this time.

"I had a German poodle named Jinx, but he died," Sabrina told us.

Emily frowned. "Don't you mean a German shepherd?" she asked.

"Nope. Jinx was a poodle, all right. My father

got him when he was in the army in Germany."

Emily made a face as if she didn't quite believe Sabrina. The face became worse when Sabrina said, "Now I have four horses."

That sounded super. "Can I come see them?" I asked.

"Well . . . I'll have to check with Justine. We're still unpacking."

"Who's Justine?"

"My mother."

"You call her Justine?" asked Marietta.

"Sure," said Sabrina. "That's her name."

"What do you call your father?"

"Jake."

Smack, smack went Erin's basketball. *Smack, smack, sprong, swish.*

"What was your last school like?" I asked.

"Bigger. We had a separate gym and auditorium, and air conditioning. My teacher was young and pretty."

There was dead silence.

Then Emily said, "Mrs. Rudolph's not young and pretty, but she's my favorite teacher in the whole school."

"Mine, too," I added, then asked, "Did you study the same subjects as here?"

"Pretty much the same." Sabrina spoke with a slight lisp, which I hadn't noticed before. "We had classes in Spanish three times a week besides."

Emily looked as if she smelled something bad,

but neither Marietta nor Margo seemed aware of Sabrina's answer. They were watching Erin, who'd tucked her basketball under one arm and was walking toward us, ready to line up to go inside.

Julius Palmenter and Peach Fuzz, whose real name is Frank Cristina, followed Erin. Peach Fuzz was wandering along as if he were daydreaming, but Julius was being his usual repulsive self.

"Can I borrow one of your sneakers?" he yelled at Erin. "I want to go fishing and my boat has a leak."

Both Erin and Peach Fuzz came to a halt when they reached the edge of our circle, but not Julius. He pushed between Emily and Margo, stopping when he faced Sabrina.

"Man! Are you ever *tall*!" he said, leaning way back as if he were staring up at the Empire State Building.

Sabrina looked down over her nose at Julius. "Not if you get up off your knees," she told him.

Everyone laughed, including Peach Fuzz, who is Julius's best friend—Julius's *only* friend. Although I laughed, too, I sensed trouble ahead. Julius was glaring at the new girl the way he'd glared at Rob just before attacking with his pencil.

I had no idea how many friends Sabrina had made that afternoon, but I knew one thing for certain. She had just made her first enemy.

2

When I met Emily at the corner of her street and mine the next morning, she looked tired and grumpy. "Happy birthday," she said, and yawned.

"What's wrong?" I asked.

"I hardly got any sleep." Emily yawned again, putting a hand in front of her mouth. "Louie whined all night. At two I got out of bed to hold him and stepped in a puddle he'd made on the floor."

When I laughed, Emily shot me a dirty look. "Sometimes I think life would be easier without pets," she said.

"No way!"

"Yeah." Emily grinned. By the time we reached the school, she was almost her normal cheerful self. We waited near the big double front doors for the bell to ring, signaling that we could enter the building.

While we were standing there, a battered old

truck pulled up in front of the entrance. It had a board fastened where the front bumper should be. A hole the size of my fist was rusted through the passenger door and another, bigger hole marred the back fender. One of the front fenders was missing entirely.

The passenger door to the truck opened, and Sabrina jumped to the ground. She was wearing jeans like the day before and a green sweatshirt the color of her eyes.

"Bye, Jake," she called. "Bye, Justine."

Although the first bell had rung, Emily and I remained where we were, staring at Sabrina and the truck. I couldn't see her mother because of sunshine reflecting off the windshield, but her father looked as if he might be tall and slender like Sabrina. He had light brown hair and a long, drooping mustache. There was a red bandana tied at the neck of his blue work shirt.

"Hi, Sabrina," I said as the rusty truck pulled away.

"Oh!" Sabrina turned bright red when she saw us. "Hi."

"Was that your parents?" asked Emily.

Sabrina nodded as we walked toward her. She stood on one foot, the other leg bent at the knee and her hands shoved into the back pockets of her jeans. "That's our old truck," she said. "They're going for feed for the horses and didn't want to get the car dirty."

"Your dad looks like a cowboy," I told her as we entered the building, Emily on one side of me, Sabrina on the other.

"He was a cowboy at Disney World," Sabrina explained.

"Before it got so boring," Emily muttered under her breath.

Since I was between them, Sabrina probably didn't hear Emily. Nevertheless, I hurried to add, "I wish my father was a cowboy. I'd love to live on a ranch and have horses."

"You can come riding with me," Sabrina offered.

"As soon as I check with Justine," Emily said in a grouchy voice. Although she spoke more loudly than before, I figured Sabrina didn't hear her this time either, since we were walking into Room 12. It was filled with noise: kids talking, books being shuffled, and desk lids being pushed open and slammed shut. I put the box of chocolate cupcakes I'd brought for my birthday treat on Mrs. Rudolph's desk, then went to my seat.

"Want to come over to my house tomorrow after school?" I said to Sabrina. "I'll ask Emily, too."

"I don't know. . . ."

"My mom can call your mother tonight," I told her, "if you give me your phone number."

"All right." Sabrina scribbled her number on a piece of paper. Then she smiled and added, "Thanks!"

I didn't have another chance to talk with Sabrina until lunch. Then I showed her where to wait in line for food, pointed out the list of rules posted next to the tray rack, and took her with me to the table where Emily and I ate with the other girls.

Sabrina didn't look pleased with the grilled cheese sandwich and tomato soup our cafeteria served for lunch, but she picked up her spoon and began to eat. She didn't seem to have anything to say to the other girls. Mostly she sat and listened to the conversation around her.

Remembering what Mrs. Rudolph had said about making Sabrina feel at home, I told her, "I'll pass out my birthday treat when we go back to our room after lunch. It's chocolate cupcakes."

"Her mom bought them at Buckeye," said Emily. "Buckeye makes the best cupcakes in the whole world!"

"Emily should know—she's tried them all," teased Marietta.

"When's your birthday?" I asked Sabrina.

"April."

"What did you take for a treat?" asked Margo.

"Nothing," said Sabrina. "At my school in Florida only the little kids brought treats for their birthdays."

In the silence that fell at our table, every little noise in the rest of the cafeteria suddenly seemed louder. Along the wall near the tray rack, the serving window to the kitchen slammed shut. At the table next to ours a third grader pretended to throw up in his soup. The kid across from him said, "Gross!"

Marietta asked, "What do you want for your birthday, Cassie?"

"A ten-speed bike." I crossed my fingers, thinking, I hope!

"I know what you're getting." Emily dipped her last bite of grilled cheese sandwich into her tomato soup. "But I'm not telling." She popped the soggy piece of sandwich into her mouth.

"I'll find out after school this afternoon anyway," I told her.

"After I walk Louie," said Emily, "I'm going to Cassie's house. I have a very special present." She grinned at me.

"She's kept me guessing for months!" I told the other girls. "It's small, but has lots of parts."

"Some from near and some from far," chanted Emily, teasing me the way she had the past few weeks. She looked across the table at Sabrina. "*My* family's been lots of places, like Washington, D.C., and Gettysburg, and the JFK Space Center. My dad says it's very important for me to go places like that." She stared at Sabrina as if daring her to disagree.

"Why?"

"Because of history. He teaches history at the high school."

"Oh," said Sabrina.

"Everybody can't go running around pretending to be a *cowboy*," Emily said in a nasty voice. "Some people have to be doctors and teachers, or work with computers, *boring* jobs like that."

I was sure Emily didn't want to start a fight, but from the way Sabrina looked at her, I was glad it was time to take our trays to the rack. I jumped up, grabbed mine, and said, "Come on, Sabrina. I'll show you where to put your trash."

During recess that afternoon, Margo told us about the modeling class she was taking in the summer. Margo was trying to convince the rest of us girls to sign up for it.

"If my family wasn't going to our cabin for the summer, I'd sign up," said Emily.

"Cassie?"

"I don't know." I wasn't interested in modeling, but I didn't want to hurt Margo's feelings.

"It's a special class for girls eleven to fourteen," she said. "What about you, Sabrina? We're going to learn about makeup, fashions, and how to walk."

"I already know how to walk."

Marietta giggled, but Margo looked confused.

"I meant how to walk gracefully," said Margo. Her dark hair lay flat against her head. Her large brown eyes were anxious. "Ms. Page also teaches proper nutrition and skin care."

"She'll have a big challenge with—" Sabrina

stopped in mid-sentence, pressing her lips to-gether.

Marietta, whose smooth, caramel-colored skin never has a blemish, gave a little sigh. Margo blushed.

Smack, smack went Erin's basketball on the court behind us. Then Sabrina said, "I'd like to sign up for the class, but I have to help with the horses all summer."

Margo brightened. "Maybe you can do both."

"Is it expensive?"

"I don't know. My mother paid."

"It doesn't matter." Sabrina gave a fake smile.

"One day over spring vacation Cassie and I went into that new beauty school at the mall," said Emily. "There were before and after pictures of their customers all over the walls."

"Remember the ugly woman who was talking to the manager?" I asked.

Emily shook her head.

"You should remember," said Sabrina.

Emily glanced at her.

"She was your mother."

Emily exploded. "You take that back!" she yelled.

"Why should I? What you said about my father during lunch wasn't very nice."

"All I said was that not everybody can be a cowboy."

"It was the way you said it."

15

The bell signaling us to line up rang, but neither Emily nor Sabrina acted as if she'd heard it. They stood glaring at each other, Emily's face flushed an angry red, Sabrina's green eyes flashing furiously.

The sound of Erin's basketball hitting the ground ceased. "What's happening?" she asked as she came to join us, spinning the ball on one finger. "Did someone say something about a cowboy?"

"Nobody said a *thing* about a cowboy," snapped Sabrina.

"I was only asking."

"Well, don't." Sabrina turned her angry green glare on Erin. She ran her eyes from the top of Erin's chestnut hair, down over her top smudged with dirt from the basketball, over her blue jeans to Erin's huge sneakers. "It's none of your business, Big Foot."

Erin's mouth dropped open. Then, clutching the basketball tight against her chest, she turned and headed toward the school. Her steps were short and stiff, not at all like her normal easy lope.

Helping Sabrina Evans make friends was going to be a lot harder than I'd thought it would be.

3

By the time school let out that afternoon, the air was warmer than it had been all day. In spite of the heat, two kids were running on the school track, one of them tall and gangly. The other boy had red hair and was wearing the bright yellow shirt I remembered seeing over my bowl of raisin bran at breakfast.

I took several steps toward home and stopped. "There's my brother," I told Emily. "He must not have gone home to take his medicine."

Emily shaded her eyes with one hand, squinting against the light. "It's Alfie, all right," she agreed. "And Joe." That's Joe Cristina, who is Peach Fuzz's younger brother.

"I'd better stop him. Running could give him an asthma attack."

"I'll go home and walk Louie," said Emily. "I have to wrap your present, too."

"See you later," I called over my shoulder as I approached the track.

Although Joe's legs are much longer, Alfie kept pace with him. Their knees lifted and fell in unison as they headed in my direction. When they saw me standing in the middle of the track, they picked up speed.

"Alfie!" I yelled as they came closer.

Alfie ran straight at me, but I stood my ground.

At the last possible moment, he swerved, putting out his arms and making a sound like an airplane as he passed.

"Go take your medicine," I shouted after him. His legs moved up and down rhythmically, his blue sneakers flashing against the dark cinders.

"Alfie!" I screamed. "Come back here!"

Alfie raised a hand to show he had heard and ran on.

My parents are always preaching to Alfie that he's old enough to take charge of his own medicine and to avoid doing the things that cause asthma attacks. Alfie might be old enough, but he sure doesn't act it. Trying to decide whether or not to rat on him, I walked slowly home.

Mom sat at the kitchen table and Dad leaned against the refrigerator, as if they were waiting for me.

"What are you doing home so early?" I asked Dad. Mom usually gets off work before school's out, but I hardly ever see my father before dinner.

"Just thought I'd stop by to check on things," he told me with a little smile. "I guess I'd better be getting back."

"Aren't you going to give me my present?" I asked, thinking that had to be the reason he was waiting for me.

"Present? What present?"

"Dad!"

Mom smiled. "Close your eyes," she said.

When I'd closed my eyes, I heard Dad leave the room. There was a squeaking, then a sort of *tick, tick, tick* sound. Unable to bear the suspense any longer, I opened my eyes.

Before me was a ten-speed bicycle, blue with a shining chrome fork and a golden chain. The bicycle had a smooth, black leather seat, an odometer, a headlight, and black foam padding over the curved handlebars.

"All the bells and whistles," said Dad. "Happy birthday, Sweet Face," he added, giving me a hug.

"Thanks!" I said. "Thank you, Mom."

"You're welcome."

The bicycle was beautiful. I was going to ask Dad to take my picture on it, but that was when Alfie arrived home.

The window over the kitchen table was open, letting in warm air as well as the chirps of birds, traffic noises from the street, a lawn mower's *whir* in the distance, and the sound Alfie made as he breathed. "Unh-hooh, unh-hooh," went Alfie as he came into the backyard.

Mom and Dad exchanged glances.

"Unh-hooh, unh-hooh." The sound went up

the back steps with Alfie, entered the house, and then came into the kitchen.

It wasn't an all-out asthma attack. Alfie wasn't red, sweating, and struggling for air as he did sometimes, but he was wheezing loudly, and he looked very guilty.

"Sit," ordered Dad, pushing out a chair.

Alfie crawled onto the chair. Then he hunched forward, placing his hands on his knees.

I knew what to do. I went to the sink, filled a big glass with water, and took it to Alfie. He swallowed small sips between wheezes.

"Have you used your Alupent?" Mom asked. Although she sounded calm, her forehead was creased with worry lines.

Alfie shook his head.

"Where is it?" demanded Dad.

"Bathroom," gasped Alfie.

"A lot of good your inhaler does sitting in the bathroom," Dad told him. "You're *supposed* to use it *before* you exercise."

As I went to get the inhaler, I heard Mom ask, "Did you take your Brethine at three?"

Feeling guilty because I hadn't forced Alfie to stop running—because I hadn't squealed on him—I found the inhaler and took it to the kitchen.

By that time Mom had Alfie's container of Brethine from the cupboard over the refrigerator and was shaking out a pill. She handed him the pill as I put the inhaler on the table near him. Alfie took his Brethine first. Then he held his inhaler to his mouth, sprayed, and took a deep breath. He made a face, then did it a second time.

We waited.

Alfie sat, wheezed, and drank his water. In a few moments, Mom and Dad began talking again. I ran my hand over the seat of my new bicycle and inspected the odometer.

Before long there was a noticeable change in Alfie's wheezing. It was as if his breaths were becoming separate instead of all running together.

The medicine was working. Undecided about whether to tell on him, I took the glass, refilled it, and brought it back to him.

"Thanks," said Alfie. The guilty expression in his eyes disappeared. They narrowed to look sly.

"Now, Alfie," said Dad, "we want to know exactly what you did to bring on the asthma attack."

"Nothing."

"You have to have done something."

"No," said Alfie. "Honest."

Dad tightened his lips and reached to straighten the knot in his tie while he considered Alfie's answers.

"What were you doing right before the asthma attack?" asked Mom.

Alfie made a couple of fake wheezes.

"Answer your mother," Dad ordered.

"It was like this," began Alfie. "I was walking

along the sidewalk with Joe, see. We were minding our own business, talking about homework, when all of a sudden this big cloud of poisonous gas came drifting along and hit us. Bam!"

Mom sighed.

"We were helpless," Alfie continued. "Joe's worse off than me. He—"

"Alfred," said Dad.

Even though I have to admit Alfie is a brat, I hate to see him in trouble. "Bye," I said, wheeling my bike out of the kitchen toward the front door. This would be a good time for me to take a test ride to Emily's house.

4

Emily was standing on the sidewalk in front of her house, waiting for me. She held Louie's leash in one hand, my birthday present in the other. The present came in a small box, wrapped in light pink paper with a big rose-colored bow.

"Lots of parts," Emily reminded me as she handed it over, "some from near and some from far." Then, her voice shaking with excitement, she added, "Open it! I can't *wait* until you see what's inside."

I untied the ribbon, peeled off the pink paper, and opened the box. A silver charm bracelet lay on a bed of white cotton.

"It's a friendship bracelet," Emily explained. "Each charm stands for something we did together."

I took the bracelet from the box and held it up. A tiny silver ballerina brought back the ballet my parents had taken Emily and me to, and a trefoil

23

stood for the years we'd been in the same Girl Scout troop. There was a small silver charm in the shape of the state of Michigan for the week I'd spent at their cabin with Emily's family, and a little bicycle that was a souvenir of all our bike trips out the trail to the abandoned farm.

When I gently touched one wheel of the bicycle, it spun beneath my finger. "Thanks, Em!" I told her. "I *love* it!"

"The map of Michigan gave me the idea. I saw it at a flea market last summer. I've been collecting the other charms ever since."

"Put it on me." I gave Emily the bracelet, then held out my wrist.

"There's space for more charms," she explained as she fastened the clasp, "for more good times together."

When I moved my arm, the charms made a tinkling sound. "I'll wear it forever," I promised. "When I'm an old lady, I'll look at it and remember how we were best friends."

"I knew you'd like it." Emily's round face was beaming with pleasure. "I saw another charm the other day, a little dog exactly like Louie. I wanted to add it to the bracelet, but I didn't have any more money."

At the sound of his name, Louie, who'd been circling Emily's feet as we talked, whined. He plumped down on his fat bottom and looked up at her.

24

"Where'd you see the charm?"

"In JCPenney at the mall." Emily untangled her legs from Louie's leash and bent to pick up the puppy. "Two weeks ago."

"Let's ride out to the mall and see if it's still there. Grandmother Ryan sent me some money for my birthday."

"Great! I'll put Louie inside and get my bike."

As I waited for Emily, I examined my new ten-speed again. It was perfect, everything I'd always wanted in a bicycle and more. I checked the bag under the seat to make certain my cable and lock were there, then pulled my money out of the zip pocket of my jacket and counted it.

"What did Alfie give you?" Emily asked when we were riding through back streets to the mall.

"Trouble," I told her, then laughed. "Alfie's the one in trouble. He wouldn't stop running and had an asthma attack, so he didn't give me a present yet. I bet it's a candy bar."

"Why?"

"That's what he gives me every year."

My new bike went like the wind. I barely had to touch the pedals and they'd spin. More than once I had to slow down for Emily to catch up with me. At the entrance to the mall, I waited with one foot on the curb to prop myself up until she rode up beside me.

"Phew!" Emily blew a stream of air from her mouth to lift the fringe of fuzzy hair falling across her forehead. "I'm going to be great on long-distance hikes this summer."

"I wish you didn't go away," I told her. "I get so lonely without you."

"Maybe you and Sabrina will end up best friends."

"Don't be silly."

"You seem pretty close already."

"I'm only trying to be a good sponsor."

Even though Emily and I locked our bicycles together and to the bike rack, too, I had a funny feeling as we walked away from them. What if we came back and my new ten-speed was gone?

I didn't need to worry. We'd just walked into the entrance of Penney's when we saw Sabrina. She was looking through a rack of ladies' nightgowns.

Emily grabbed me by one arm and tried to drag me down a different aisle, but she was too late. The words were already out of my mouth.

"Hi, Sabrina," I said.

"Hi." Sabrina smiled at us, then glanced at the nightgowns. "We were too busy packing before we moved for me to shop for a Mother's Day present, so I'm looking for one now."

"That's pretty." As I reached to touch a pale yellow gown, the charms on my bracelet tinkled. "Oh! Look at what Emily gave me for my birthday!" I lifted my arm so Sabrina could see. "It's a friendship bracelet. Isn't it beautiful?"

Then I glanced at Emily. Her face wore the same expression it had the day Julius Palmenter threw her science project into a snowbank on the way to school.

"We're going to see if Penney's has a charm of a puppy," I said to Sabrina. "If you want—"

"I just remembered," Emily interrupted. "My mother told me to wait until she came home before I went anywhere."

"But . . ." I looked from Emily to Sabrina and back again.

"I'd better go home right now." Emily moved away. "Come on, Cassie," she said.

"See you tomorrow," I told Sabrina.

I caught up with Emily as she reached the bike rack. "That was rude," I told her, "and it wasn't true, either. Your mother didn't tell you to stay home."

"How do you know?"

Emily sounded so angry I fumbled at my combination lock and had to start dialing again. "You were coming over to my house," I said.

"So I told a white lie. Big deal. I didn't want Sabrina butting in on us."

"She wasn't butting in. I spoke first."

"I wish you didn't."

"Mrs. Rudolph made me Sabrina's sponsor," I pointed out.

"So what? I don't like Sabrina and I don't want to go anyplace with her."

"But, Emily," I protested. "I invited Sabrina to my house tomorrow, and I already told her I'd ask you, too."

"Then you can just uninvite her."

"I can't!" I wailed.

As the cable fell free, Emily grabbed her bicycle. She jerked it out of the rack and wheeled it into a backward turn to face the street. "You decided all by yourself that I'd be perfectly happy to sit around listening to Sabrina brag." Emily's blue eyes were fierce, her voice tense with anger. "You didn't even *ask* me first!"

"I—"

"Well, you can count me out. I don't like your sneaking around, buttering up Sabrina."

"I'm not sneaking!"

"And if you want to be my best friend, Cassie Ryan," said Emily as she swung onto her bike seat, "you won't hang around with Sabrina Evans!"

5

I was hoping Emily would change her mind by the next day, but she didn't. She hardly spoke to me on the way to school. During lunch and recess, she practically ignored me, and she acted as if Sabrina wasn't there at all.

On the way home that afternoon I walked between them, Sabrina next to the curb, and Emily on the inside. When we came to her street, I said, "Come on over to my house after you walk Louie. Please, Emily."

Emily only tossed her head and stalked away without saying good-bye. She didn't look back, either. I watched until she ran up the steps to her house, then walked on with Sabrina.

"She sure is grouchy," Sabrina commented.

"Emily's a little bit moody," I admitted, "but she's a super person."

Sabrina made a noise. I wasn't certain if it meant she agreed with me or not. "My mother's usually

home from work when I get home from school,"
I said. "She has to take my brother for new shoes,
but she wanted to meet you first."

As we entered the front door, I shouted, "I'm
home!"

"I'm in the kitchen," Mom answered.

That was fine with me, since the kitchen is one
of my favorite places in our house. The walls are
painted the same bright yellow as smily faces, and
the color of the floor and cupboards reminds me
of butterscotch candy. On the table in front of the
window are the hen and rooster salt and pepper
shakers I used to play with when I was little. That
afternoon a green glass holding three red tulips sat
beside the rooster.

"I'm so glad you could come home with
Cassie," Mom said when I introduced Sabrina.
Her smile spread wide across her face. "I know
you will be great friends."

"Can we have birthday cake?" I asked.

"Help yourselves. There are apples and grapes,
too."

While I divided the cake, Mom mixed a can of
mushroom soup into a casserole she was preparing
for dinner. She was setting the dials on the oven
when Sabrina and I headed upstairs.

"Tell Alfie I'm ready to take him for shoes,"
Mom called after me. "He's up in his room, doing
his breathing exercises."

Alfie was in his room, but he wasn't doing his

breathing exercises. He was sitting on his bed, eating a chocolate bar and reading *Supersnoop*, his favorite comic book. He looked up at Sabrina and me, then down again.

"Mom's ready to go to the store," I told him.

Sabrina put her backpack and plate of cake on my bed, then crossed to the shelves where I keep my stuffed animals. She picked up the polar bear in a red ski sweater Dad gave me for Valentine's Day. "Do you like having a little brother?" she asked.

"Sometimes."

Sabrina put down the bear to pick up the Shamu I'd bought on a visit to Sea World.

"He's a brat," I said.

"He didn't seem so bad." Sabrina abandoned Shamu to examine the animals on the bottom shelf. "You have more stuffed animals than Kmart," she said.

"I collect them." I pointed to a black cat with white paws. "That looks exactly like Mittsey, the cat across the street."

"Guess who this looks like." Sabrina held up the pink piggy who sits next to the cat.

"Who?"

"That kid who hangs around with Julius."

I snorted, then laughed, because the pig really did resemble Peach Fuzz. They had the same round stomach, pinkish skin, and innocent blue eyes. The pig even had yellowish bristles of hair

31

on top of his head, where the pink had faded.

"Your room is beautiful," Sabrina said as she put the piggy back.

"Thanks." My eyes followed hers as they looked around. Last summer Mom and I had painted the walls and ceiling white, and the bed, dresser, and shelves blue. We'd found a dark blue spread with a long ruffle clear to the floor in the Sears catalog. There were white ruffled throw pillows leaning against the head of the bed, and a matching blue ruffled pillow on the seat of the white wicker rocker near the dresser.

Sabrina and I sat on the bed to eat our cake, her cross-legged next to her backpack, me propped up against the headboard with pillows. In a little while Mom came to the bottom of the steps and yelled for Alfie. A few seconds later we heard the sound of his feet thundering down the steps.

I ran a finger around the edge of my plate to wipe up the remaining icing, then licked the finger clean. "I used to collect stickers, too," I told her, "but I forgot and left them out back on the picnic table one night last summer. It rained and by morning they were all stuck together."

"I collect postcards." Sabrina licked a crumb from the corner of her mouth. "I have cards from forty-two states, from London, England, and from Germany."

"How many in all?"

"Two hundred and three. I have forty-four from San Francisco."

"Did you live there?"

"No." Sabrina looked away from me, at the empty plate she was holding.

I hopped up to take the plates to my dresser. As I crawled back on the bed, I asked, "Who sends you the cards?"

"Just somebody." Sabrina's *s*'s whistled. "Nobody important." She pulled her backpack close, hugging it tightly to her stomach. Her long black curls fell forward across her face, hiding her expression from me.

All that made me really curious about Sabrina's postcards and especially about who sent them, but there was no way I could ask without being pushy. I said, "We can play video games if you want."

Sabrina's grip on her backpack loosened. "Let's read my welcome notes first," she said. "They're still in here from yesterday." She took a tablet and her science book from the pack, then upended it. Papers flew everywhere, turning my dark blue spread into a crazy quilt.

I reached to grab a paper covered by a large scrawl. "This is mine," I told her. "Keep it for last."

Sabrina sorted through the notes, picking one on yellow paper. " 'Dear Sabrina,' " she read. " 'Welcome to Oakway. I'm glad you're here because I'm sick of the same old faces. Totally cool,

Rob.' " She looked over the note at me. "Who's Rob?"

"The boy with the big ears who sits in back of Julius. He thinks he's a big deal."

Sabrina read a couple more notes out loud, then one that said, " 'Good to have you here. Go, Browns!' " She held the note out for me to see. "Instead of signing it, this person made a weird drawing."

"That's a dog bone."

"A *dog* bone?"

Sabrina sounded so repulsed I laughed. "The dog bone's the symbol for the Cleveland Browns's defense team," I told her. "Peach Fuzz must have written it. He's the only kid I know who wears orange and brown all year in honor of the Browns."

Sabrina read more notes aloud before picking up a tightly folded square of paper and opening it. "Look at this." She placed the paper between us, smoothing it flat.

I AM glAD YOU

CAME TO ☒ AhE SCHOOl

Julius

"It looks like a ransom note," she said.

After Julius's note, the only ones left were Emily's and mine. Sabrina picked up Emily's.

" 'Dear Sabrina Evans,' " she read. " 'I'm glad you came to our class because there are more boys than girls in Room 12 and you will help even things out. Also, you are very pretty and I think you are nice, too.' "

My fingers went to my charm bracelet. "Emily wants to be friends," I told Sabrina. "She wouldn't have written that you're pretty and nice if she didn't."

"She wrote the note before she knew me."

That was when I realized how important it was to me that Sabrina and Emily liked each other. How could I be friends with both of them if they hated each other? "Emily doesn't know you now, either," I said. "You two just got off to a bad start."

"Maybe," said Sabrina, but she sounded as if she meant, "Oh, yeah?"

"Don't forget my note." I gave it to her.

Sabrina read silently at first, then out loud. " 'We can ride our bicycles out the Iron Horse Trail. You can sleep over at my house, and we'll go on hikes and swimming together.' " She lifted her head to look at me. "You mean that?"

"Sure," I said, trying to sound as positive as I could. Sabrina was so pretty, and so different from the other girls. Beside her, they seemed almost ordinary. I *did* want to be her friend, but I kept hearing Emily's voice in my mind. "If you want to be my best friend, Cassie Ryan," it said, "you won't hang around with Sabrina Evans!"

6

"Our spring play will be presented the Friday morning before Memorial Day," Mrs. Rudolph announced the next day before lunch. She handed a stack of papers to the first person in each row. In my row Margo took one and gave the rest of the papers to Peach Fuzz, who passed them to Sabrina, who passed them to me. I began reading as I passed the last sheet of paper over my shoulder to Josh: "Give me your tired, your poor. . . ."

"The poem you are holding was written by Emma Lazarus," Mrs. Rudolph told us. "Does anyone know where those words appear? Erin?"

"On the base of the Statue of Liberty."

"Very good," said Mrs. Rudolph. "Tryouts for the play are next Wednesday after school in the gym. If you want a speaking part, bring the poem to read aloud."

Chris's hand went up. "Yes, Chris?" Mrs. Rudolph asked.

"How many people in the play?"

"The largest single role is that of the Statue of Liberty, who will be on stage for the entire play, but there are some larger and smaller speaking parts for both boys and girls. In addition, we'll need a lot of people for immigrants."

I finished the poem and glanced at Emily, who was still reading. I could see myself standing center stage, head high, Liberty's light held proudly aloft. The only obstacle I could think of is the fact that I am very short.

Just then, Julius burst into the room. He hadn't been at school all morning, which was nothing unusual.

"Do you have a note for me, Julius?" Mrs. Rudolph asked.

Julius shook his head.

"Figures," said Rob.

"I don't want to hear that kind of talk, Rob," Mrs. Rudolph told him. "It isn't funny and it isn't smart, either." She looked at Julius, then at our class. "I want everyone to know that I think Julius is a fine person. Any day he comes to school is a good day for me."

It wasn't strange that Mrs. Rudolph said that, since she was probably trying to make Julius feel good. The weird thing was, the way Mrs. Rudolph spoke left no doubt she was telling the absolute truth. She really *was* glad when Julius showed up in the morning.

Sometimes Mrs. Rudolph is very difficult to figure out.

When we lined up to go out for recess that afternoon, Mrs. Rudolph told Sabrina and Erin to walk together. She had Margo walk with Emily and Marietta with me. "You don't always have to associate with the same people," she told us. "Life's more interesting with a variety of friends."

I agreed with her, although I wondered what Emily was thinking. I found out when she raised her hand and protested, "But Mrs. Rudolph, you matched us up by height!"

"Practically everyone in the entire school is taller than I am," I complained to Marietta when we'd reached the playground.

"I'm not," she said.

"I hate going through life looking up at people!"

"It won't always be like that," said Marietta. "The other kids got their growth early. In a couple of years we'll be staring down at the tops of their heads."

"You think?"

"I *know*." Marietta smiled proudly. "I have Watusi blood. My mother's five ten and my father's six four. Maybe some of your ancestors were tall, too."

"I doubt it. My mother looks me right in the eye and my dad's only five eight."

Except for Erin, who was dribbling under the basket, the other girls reached the tree before us. As we joined them, Margo was saying, "It would be just like Mrs. Rudolph to give Julius a part in the play. If she does, I'm not going to be in it.

Julius is nothing but trouble."

"Don't worry," said Emily. "Nobody in their right mind would let Julius Palmenter up on stage in front of the whole school, not even Mrs. Rudolph."

"I'm going to try out for the part of Lady Liberty," said Sabrina, who'd brought the poem out to recess with her. She was wearing jeans and her green sweatshirt again, but that day she'd combed her hair back. It was gathered at the nape of her neck and held by a green ribbon tied in a floppy bow.

"So am I," said Margo. "Ms. Page says it's important for self-confidence to get used to being in front of people."

Sabrina stared at the paper she was holding. "Listen," she said, then read the poem slowly and carefully.

As she read, I realized there would be no way Sabrina could capture the starring role. Maybe it was because she was trying so hard, but Sabrina's lisp had become very noticeable.

"How'd I sound?" she asked when she'd finished.

"Okay," said Marietta.

Sabrina frowned.

"It sounded good to me," Margo told her.

"Is there any way I can improve?"

When Emily opened her mouth—probably to say something like "Disappear"—I hurried to speak first. "It's perfect except for your lisp."

"What lisp?" Sabrina scowled, drawing her dark eyebrows together.

"Most of the time it's barely noticeable," I told her. "Maybe when—"

Sabrina didn't let me finish my sentence. "Are *you* trying out for Lady Liberty?" she asked.

"Yes." The Statue of Liberty stood on a base. My father could build me a high base so it wouldn't matter that I'm short.

"Then you can forget all about that part, Sabrina," Emily said cheerfully. "Cassie's a cinch for it."

"Why?"

"Experience."

"I've had experience, too. I was substitute for Bo Peep in Nurseryland Village near Disney World."

"Cassie was Mary in her church play at Christmas," said Marietta.

"*And* she had the starring role in our school play last spring," Emily added.

Smack went Erin's basketball as she dribbled. *Smack, smack.* Julius and Peach Fuzz, who'd been yelling comments at her as she practiced, drifted closer to us girls.

"What was the play?" Sabrina asked me.

"Scenes from *Charlotte's Web.*"

"You were Charlotte?" As Sabrina's green eyes examined me, they grew thoughtful.

"Yes."

"You must have been typecast."

40

"What's typecast?" asked Marietta.

Sabrina shrugged, the movement graceful. "It's when a director gives a part to an actor because that person fits the role physically," she explained. "Charlotte had to be someone small and dark, with a biggish stomach and skinny arms and legs for—"

"Wait a minute!" I yelled.

"A spider," she finished.

Julius snickered. Erin's ball made one last smack. She stopped dribbling to stare in our direction.

"That's dumb," I said. I'd never even heard of typecasting.

Sabrina smiled at me, but it wasn't a nice smile. "It's too bad this year's play isn't *Snow White and the Seven Dwarfs*," she said. "There'd be lots of parts for you."

Julius gave a catcall, then laughed out loud, making a big production of it. He grabbed his stomach and bent double.

Peach Fuzz slapped Julius on the back and laughed, too, but none of the girls did. Margo began nibbling on a hangnail. Marietta looked angry, and Emily had a strange little smile on her face.

I opened my mouth, hoping for a really big put-down to come out, but none did. While I stood with it hanging open, Julius straightened.

"Da-da, da-da, da-da, da-da," he sang to the tune of *Batman* on TV. "*Spiderwoman!*"

41

7

As soon as I walked in the house, I knew it was no time to complain to Mom about my new nickname. When she's in a bad mood, Mom bakes a cake, beating the batter by hand with a large wooden spoon. When I entered the kitchen, she was standing at the counter, one hand steadying a big yellow bowl, the other wielding the spoon.

"Sixty-six, sixty-seven," she said.

"Hi, Mom," I said.

"Hello. Sixty-nine and seventy, and . . ."

"Dad home yet?" I asked hopefully. Dad would tell me I was beautiful if I looked like the Loch Ness monster.

"No. Seventy-two."

"Where's Alfie?"

Mom's eyes left the cake batter to meet mine. She was in a bad mood, all right. "In his room," she said. "Eighty-six and . . ."

"Thanks," I told her, deciding not to mention she'd skipped fourteen seconds.

I ran upstairs. Alfie'd tell me I had no resemblance to a spider. He can be totally honest when it doesn't cost him anything.

Alfie was sprawled flat on his bed, face-down, his forehead resting on one arm. Although his straight red hair fell forward to hide his face, I could see his throat move as he swallowed. His room smelled strongly of chocolate.

"Oh, good," he said, relief crossing his face when he looked up and saw me. "I thought you were Mom."

"Why's she mad?"

"She went past the school on the way home from work and caught me running track."

I cocked an ear to his breathing. "You sound okay to me."

"I didn't get a single lap in." Alfie sat up, folded his arms across his chest, and tried to look indignant. "How'll I pass the fitness test for spy school if I'm not allowed to do P.T.?"

"P.T.?"

"Physical training."

"You can swim at the Y," I pointed out, "and run track when it's not the pollen season."

Alfie brought his knees up to rest his arms on them. "I'm a prisoner in my own room, in my own *body*," he said in a somber voice, "but someday everyone will recognize my power. I'll go to the defense of my country, enlist as a master spy for the United States of America." His eyes glistened, and he forgot to sound gloomy. "I'll fight the forces of evil, track down the enemies of our nation, uncover their crimes, risk—"

"I have an important question," I interrupted. "Promise you'll give the first answer that pops into your head, so I'll know it's the truth."

"All right," agreed Alfie, abandoning his description of himself as a national hero. "Ask me anything."

"Do I look like a spider?"

"Of course not."

I heaved a sigh of relief.

"You only have four arms and legs. Spiders have six." Alfie wrinkled his forehead as if he were concentrating on a difficult math problem. "Or is it eight?"

I said a word I'm not supposed to know, let alone repeat in public.

"I'll tell!" Alfie bounded off his bed. "I'll tell Mom! You said— Ulp!"

I caught him before he reached the door, clamped a hand over his mouth, and dragged him back onto his bed. "If you say one word," I threatened, "I'll squeal that you were pigging out on that chocolate you're allergic to."

Since my hand was clamped tight against his lips, Alfie couldn't answer. His eyes bugged out.

Loosening my grip, I hissed, "Blink twice if you agree on a pact of silence."

Alfie held out a little longer, then blinked twice.

I let go of him to sit up.

"Urggle," said Alfie, rubbing dramatically at his neck.

"I always thought my biggest physical imperfection was that mole on my left cheek where a dimple should be," I said.

"You mean that brown dot Mom calls a beauty mark?"

I nodded. "Then today during recess I found out I look like a spider." I glanced down at my stomach. It wasn't *that* big.

"Why do you think you look like a spider?" Alfie asked, still rubbing at his neck.

"Sabrina said so. Julius and Peach Fuzz heard her." I shuddered, remembering. "Now Julius is calling me Spiderwoman."

Alfie rubbed harder.

"Stop that," I ordered. "You'll make your neck red and I'll get the blame."

"I heard something about Sabrina," he told me. "Mom and Dad were talking and her name came up."

"When?" Alfie and his friend Joe are always spying on people. They spy on Emily and me, on Julius and Peach Fuzz, and on Mom and Dad. Maybe Alfie heard something useful.

"The night of your birthday. I was in the bathroom pretending to wash my hands. It was kind of hard to hear with the water running, but I managed."

"What did they say?"

"What's it worth?"

"A Hershey's bar."

"What size?"

"Four ounce."

Alfie tilted his head and narrowed his eyes as if considering the offer. Then he said, "Deal."

"So what did they say?"

"Nothing much. Mom was telling Dad that she got to talking to Sabrina's mother when she called her. You know, to say it was okay for Sabrina to come over."

"For this I have to pay a Hershey's bar?"

"Wait a second," said Alfie. "No. Mom said the lady mentioned Sabrina was her *stepdaughter*."

That wasn't much better. "Anything else?" I asked.

Alfie shook his head. "That's all. Dad pounded on the bathroom door and yelled at me to stop wasting water."

When I sighed, Alfie asked me, "Why do you want information about Sabrina?"

"Because I volunteered to be her sponsor, to help her fit in, but she keeps making all the other girls mad. I thought we'd be good friends, maybe hang around together this summer, but now I'm starting to be sorry she ever moved here." I looked at Alfie. A smudge of chocolate on his lower lip reminded me of our agreement.

"Your information isn't worth a four-ounce candy bar," I told him.

"A deal's a deal."

"All right," I agreed, "but you'll have to wait for delivery until I go to the store."

"Don't bother," said Alfie. "I figure we're even."

"Why?"

"I just ate your birthday present."

8

When Mrs. Rudolph asked for volunteers to make play posters during recess Monday, I raised my hand right away. I love the workroom, with its huge rolls of colored construction paper and generous supply of crayons and paints. I even like the smell of paste.

I was glad when Emily volunteered, and right after her, Marietta and Margo. Erin kept her hand down since she never gives up basketball practice unless she's forced to.

Unfortunately, right after calling on the four of us, Mrs. Rudolph added, "And Sabrina. Cassie can show you where the supplies are kept."

"Spiderwoman," Julius whispered as I passed near him on my way out of the room. I didn't need him to remind me of Sabrina's sharp tongue. I'd already felt a sinking sensation at the sound of her name.

While Margo, Marietta, and Emily assembled poster paper and paints on the long table in the center of the workroom, I showed Sabrina where the scissors and pencils were kept and how to remove construction paper from the large rolls.

Sabrina nodded. She'd been very quiet all day. Maybe she'd decided her big mouth had gotten her into enough trouble already.

When Sabrina and I joined the other girls at the worktable, Emily had already drawn several letters on her poster, and Marietta was penciling in figures of people. Margo was using tempera, painting large letters directly onto the paper without using lines to guide her. She left a space after each black letter.

"I'm painting a little red flower between each letter," she explained.

"All my letters are going to be small, at the bottom of the poster," Marietta said, as much to herself as to the rest of us. "I'm putting the Statue of Liberty on the right side of the poster, with a Russian gymnast, a Japanese computer engineer, and an African princess walking toward Lady Liberty from the left."

"What does a Japanese computer engineer look like?" asked Emily.

"Smart." Marietta straightened to examine her drawing. "I'm dressing as an African princess for the play," she said. "My dad's taking a personal day from work so he can videotape the whole thing to show at our family reunion this summer."

"If I give you a blank tape, will he copy it for me?" I asked, thinking I'd like a video of me as

Lady Liberty and of all the other kids in costume.

"Sure. Do you want one, Margo? Emily?"

When they agreed, Marietta asked, very politely, "What about you, Sabrina?"

"Probably not."

"It's just a school play," Emily said sarcastically. "It's not important, like being Bo Peep at Nurseryland Village."

Although I saw Sabrina's hurt look, I didn't think to hold back the question I'd planned for her.

"What did you get Justine for Mother's Day?" I asked, leading up to it.

"A nightgown."

"I always have a terrible time picking out a gift for my mother," I went on. "And I only have to buy one. It must be really hard to decide on two, or did you buy your real mother the same thing you got Justine?"

Sabrina went very still, her hand frozen in the act of reaching for a paintbrush. As she moved again to pick up the brush, she said, "I only bought one. My real mother is dead."

"Oh," I said. "I'm sorry."

Sabrina shrugged. "I was a little kid when she died. I barely remember her."

"I have a stepmother, too," said Margo, "but I live with my mom and my big brother."

Sabrina's green eyes darted at Margo, then back at her poster. "I'm lucky," she said. "Justine picked me for a daughter. Most mothers are stuck with the kids they bring home from the hospital."

"I figure Justine wanted to marry your father and you came as part of the deal," Emily told her.

Sabrina looked irritated. "I *was* part of the deal," she said. "Jake would *never* give me up for any reason. He's told me that lots of times." She lisped, the way she had when she read the poem during recess.

"So Justine's stuck with you," said Emily.

I wanted to stop them, but I didn't know how. I sat there, wishing that Emily and Sabrina would shut up, or that I'd been absent, or I'd fallen asleep and dreamed the whole thing.

"At least Justine got someone pretty," said Sabrina. "She could have ended up with a kid with frizzy yellow hair, orange spots all over her face, and a shape like the Pillsbury Dough Girl."

Emily made a coughing sound.

I shut my eyes, but I couldn't shut my ears.

"You know what I think?" asked Emily.

"I don't *care* what you think."

"That your real mother isn't dead," said Emily. "I bet she ran away from home because she couldn't stand you."

Sabrina drew her breath in sharply, as if Emily had slapped her. I cautiously opened my eyes.

"That's a lie!" Sabrina told her. "My real mother's dead!"

Margo giggled nervously.

"You think that's funny?" Sabrina turned on Margo.

51

Margo shook her head, but Sabrina didn't pay any attention. She jumped to her feet, jarring the table and causing a wash of black tempera to splash across Margo's poster. "You're all a bunch of stuck-up, bragging snobs!" she yelled. "As if you have anything to brag about!"

Her green eyes jumped from one girl to the next as she spoke. "Margo, zit champion of the universe; and Marietta—Oakway Elementary's *video princess*." She glared at Emily. "The Pillsbury Dough Girl." Her voice shaking and her lisp very pronounced, Sabrina turned on me. "You're just like the rest of them, Cassie, only worse. You pretend to be my friend when you don't care about me at all."

I was so shocked I couldn't think of a thing to say. As I sat there feeling numb, Sabrina added, "I hate all of you and I hate this nerdy school!" Then she turned and ran from the workroom.

Across from me, Emily's mouth and shoulders sagged. Even the pink bow in her hair looked depressed. Tears formed in Margo's eyes. They spilled over, running down her cheeks to drip off her chin.

Marietta put an arm around Margo and hugged her. "It's all right," Marietta said, but it wasn't. It wasn't all right at all.

"Sabrina Evans is the queen of put-down," declared Emily. "I wish she'd go back to Florida and stay there!"

9

Most of the time my family has dinner together at the big round table in our dining room. In a lot of ways this is the best part of the day. I get to eat, which is one of my favorite activities, and I can sit and daydream while Mom's and Dad's voices make a comforting background rumble.

At first, dinner that evening was no different from any other day. Dad talked about what had happened at his job. I didn't listen since I wasn't much interested. I was thinking that Emily and I could ride our bicycles out the Iron Horse Trail Saturday. We could take a picnic to eat under the old apple tree on the abandoned farm. If we were lucky, we might spot the muskrat that lives in a nearby pond.

Then Mom began telling Dad something that brought me to the present with a jolt. She was talking about Justine Evans—Sabrina's step-mother.

"Justine wanted to know if I could recommend a good furnace man," Mom told him. "Then she invited me out to their place Saturday. Evidently, the house needs a lot of work, but they plan to do most of the repairs themselves."

Dad made a noncommittal sound as he took a bite of chicken, not his favorite food.

"They have to have a new furnace installed," Mom went on, "but the rest of the house can wait until everything else is finished."

"A farm's a lot of work," Dad observed.

"Please pass the salt," said Alfie. He was carefully moving his peas to one side of his plate so they didn't touch his chicken or french fries.

"It isn't a farm," said Mom as she passed the salt. "It's— Alfie! Use your fork, not your fingers, to eat your french fries."

"What's for dessert?" asked Alfie.

"Ice cream," Mom told him, "but only after you finish your vegetables."

"I think I'm allergic to peas." Alfie rubbed vigorously at a raised red area above one bony wrist. "They give me hives."

"That's an insect bite," said Mom.

"It wasn't there before I ate the peas."

"The point is," Dad informed him, "you haven't eaten any peas yet."

Alfie frowned at the small green vegetables on his plate, then brightened. "It was probably the pea pollen that caused it."

"Alfred—"

54

"I'm eating them. I'm eating them!" Alfie took two peas on a spoon, swallowed them, then quickly drank water. He shut his eyes tightly and shuddered.

"What did you say her last name is?" Dad asked Mom.

Since Mom had to finish chewing before she answered, I said, "Is there any chance we're related to the Watusi?" In the past week Marietta seemed to have grown taller. Soon I'd be the shortest person in our class.

"Who's Watusi?" Alfie demanded.

"An African tribe of very tall people," Dad explained.

"It sounds like the name of that kid in kindergarten," said Alfie. "When me and Joe catch that kid . . ." He paused to consider.

"Evans," said Mom. "Justine Evans."

"We aren't related to the Watusi," Dad told me. "If we were, you'd be taller."

Alfie made a fist and shook his skinny arm above the table. "Boom!" he said. "Right in the kisser! There'll be nothing left but blood and a pile of broken bones."

"Cassie's invited, too," said Mom, "since she and Sabrina are such good friends."

I choked.

"Don't eat so fast," Mom told me. "Justine thought you girls could get together while she and I visit."

"I don't want to get together," I protested. "I

decided I don't like her. Nobody does."

"That's not a very nice thing to say."

"It's the truth."

"Sabrina seemed fine the day she was here," Mom pointed out.

"That was before anybody knew what she's really like."

"Don't be so negative."

"And what is she really like?" asked Dad, an edge to his voice.

"She thinks she's better than we are. She said Emily's shaped like the Pillsbury Dough Girl, and that Margo's the zit champion of the universe. She told me I only got my part in *Charlotte's Web* because I look like a spider. Sabrina says she hates all of us and she hates our nerdy school."

"Oh, dear," said Mom.

"Want me and Joe to get her?" asked Alfie.

"Thanks." I smiled at him. "I'm sorry I offered to trade you for a golden retriever."

"You will not *get* anybody," Dad told Alfie. "You will sit there and eat your peas like a gentleman."

"I don't want to be a gentleman," said Alfie.

"Eat!" roared Dad.

"I already told Justine we'd be there," Mom said in worried tones.

"Terrific." For a second I thought my peas, chicken, and french fries would make a return appearance on the dinner table.

"And you will be there," Dad ordered. "You

will go, act civilized, and thank the girl when you leave."

"Yes, sir," I said, wondering how I could keep this visit to Sabrina secret from Emily and the other girls.

10

At lunch on Wednesday, the rest of us talked about play tryouts and the parts we wanted, but Sabrina didn't say a word. Later, she must have made an excuse to stay in from recess, and she didn't show up for tryouts either.

Every other girl in Room 12 reported to the gym after school. Most of the boys were there, too, except for Julius. He'd gotten into a fight during recess and ended up in the principal's office. He was still sitting beside the secretary's desk when Emily and I walked by after dismissal.

Nine boys read for speaking parts, including Peach Fuzz. "Don't go away," Mrs. Rudolph told them when they'd finished. "Parts will be assigned at the end of tryouts."

The first girl to read was Margo.

"She'll never be Lady Liberty," said Emily. "Statues don't get zits."

I figured Emily was right, but not because of

Margo's zits. Margo broke into giggles right in the middle of the poem.

Erin was next. She was plenty loud and she didn't giggle, but it's hard to imagine Lady Liberty with orange sneakers sticking out from under the hem of her robe. Just the same, Erin was better than Margo—until the last line.

" 'I lift my lamp beside the golden door!' " Erin finished in ringing tones. She swept her right arm into the air and rose up on her toes, looking exactly as if she were going for a jump shot.

I was the last girl to try out. My voice shook a little, but I'd memorized the poem and I didn't leave anything out. When I went back to the gym floor, Emily made an "okay" sign and said, "I know you'll get it!"

I hoped so. I waited nervously as Mrs. Rudolph climbed the four steps to the stage. "Deciding on speaking roles was very difficult," she told us, "because there are a lot of talented people in this room. And I want you to know we need every one of you to make our play a success."

She looked at the yellow pad she'd been making notes on. "Beth Anne is the Irish lassie, and Marietta is our African princess," she said, then assigned the parts of the Greek and Russian immigrants and the ship's captain to kids in Miss Foster's room. "Our tugboat skipper is Frank," said Mrs. Rudolph, meaning Peach Fuzz. "Margo is Lady Liberty—"

"I don't believe it!" Margo screamed. She jumped up and down, her hands clasped in front of her. "I don't believe it!"

"Believe it," Mrs. Rudolph told her. "And the role of Emma Lazarus goes to Cassie Ryan."

"Wretched refuse again," muttered Emily, who'd been a discarded popcorn box in the skit for Community Cleanup Day.

"People with speaking parts report here after school tomorrow," Mrs. Rudolph reminded us. Then she added, "Cassie, will you please meet me in our homeroom? I want to talk with you privately."

I told Emily I'd see her later, and went to Room 12. On the table behind our desks, Speedy, one of the gerbils, ran in his wheel. Big Momma was sleeping on a mound of wood chips. I took a chair from the table and put it next to Mrs. Rudolph's desk.

When she arrived, Mrs. Rudolph put her yellow pad on the desk, but held onto her pencil, tapping it on the pad as we talked. "Sabrina doesn't seem very happy," she said. "Is there a problem with the other girls?"

"They don't like her."

"They don't?" Mrs. Rudolph sounded surprised.

"She's always bragging about her school in Florida. She brags about her parents, too."

"Maybe she doesn't have anything you girls are familiar with to talk about."

"She calls the other kids names," I said. "She called Emily the Pillsbury Dough Girl."

Tap went Mrs. Rudolph's pencil. *Tap, tap.* Then she said, "Sometimes it's when we aren't acting nice that we need friends the most."

I shifted on my chair. "Being friendly toward Sabrina is like hugging a cactus," I told her. "Every time we get near, she jabs us."

Mrs. Rudolph stopped tapping the pencil. "And you don't like prickly?" she said with a twinkle in her eye.

I saw her point—*Emily* is prickly. Avoiding her eyes, I looked at the big red ceramic apple sitting on her desk next to a stack of test papers. The apple had a bright green worm sticking out from its smooth surface. In the hall, the maintenance man's bucket made a clanking sound. Somewhere a door slammed.

"It's very difficult to fit in at a new school," Mrs. Rudolph said, "especially near the end of the year when friendships are already solid. It can be horribly lonely."

I swallowed. I knew all about lonely.

"But I don't want being Sabrina's sponsor to be a burden to you," Mrs. Rudolph added in a soft voice. "If you want, I can relieve you of the responsibility."

I shook my head. I couldn't do that to anyone, not even Sabrina.

"Are you certain?"

Although I wasn't, I said, "Yes."

"Good for you," said Mrs. Rudolph. "Sabrina might be prickly, but she needs your friendship."

When I left Room 12, the only other person in the hall was Mr. Harris, our maintenance man. He was outside the boys' lavatory, holding the door open with one hand. "What are you boys doing in there?" he demanded of someone inside.

"Washing our hands," said a voice like Julius Palmenter's.

"Go wash them at home. School's been dismissed for over an hour."

"I was at play tryouts," said another voice, which I recognized as belonging to Peach Fuzz.

"Those are finished, too. Are you going to leave, or do I have to report you to the principal?"

I'd passed the boys' lavatory and was walking by the girls' room when the door swung open and Sabrina emerged. Her face turned red when she saw me.

"Hi, Sabrina," I said, trying to sound cheerful. "Why didn't you try out for the play?"

"I had a stomachache." Sabrina glanced over her shoulder at Mr. Harris. "Did you know when it's real quiet in there you can hear what they're saying in the boys' room?"

"I've never been in the girls' room when it's quiet."

"Oh," said Sabrina. Then she added, "I don't know who I was listening to."

"Julius and Peach Fuzz," I told her, "planning trouble as usual."

We left the building by the front entrance. Parked outside was the Evans's battered old truck. Sabrina ran toward it.

"Bye," I called as she climbed inside. "See you tomorrow."

"Good-bye." As the truck passed me, Sabrina turned toward the window, her lips curved into an uncertain smile.

11

At first I thought no one was home, but then I spotted a pair of legs sticking out from under the yew bush in our front yard. I was fairly certain the legs belonged to my brother, but I bent over to check anyway.

Alfie was lying on his belly in the dirt and dry yew needles. He held a cardboard tube from a roll of paper towels to one eye.

"Where's Mom?" I asked.

"She had to go to the store."

"You know you're not supposed to lie in the grass, Alfie," I told him.

"Alfie's a baby name," he said. "Call me Al."

"What are you doing, Al?"

"Practicing my spying."

I flopped beside him, then looked in the direction the tube was aimed. All I could see was the street and Mr. Detreich and Mittsey on the other side. Mittsey was sitting on the porch washing one of her white paws while Mr. Detreich watered his azalea bushes. His tubby figure moved slowly, stopping to give each bush a drink.

"I hate to tell you, Al, but you'll never be a spy."

"Why not?" Alfie asked in an uninterested tone as he moved the tube to match Mr. Detreich's progress along the row of bushes.

"Your red hair is very noticeable. You'd be spotted and tortured by the enemy before you uncovered any of their secrets."

"I'd be too valuable to torture. My side will pay millions to get me back."

"Besides," I continued, "in pollen season you always start wheezing. The other spies would hear you coming."

Alfie took the tube from his eye to look at me. There was a round red circle where he'd pressed it against his skin. The whole effect resembled a target with a brown bull's-eye.

"You think I'll hang around fields, spying on cows?" he asked scornfully. "I'm going to be a city spy. There aren't any pollens in the city."

"What are you spying on now?"

"The trail to Joe's house. Me and him were supposed to make contact at four sixteen." Alfie checked his watch. "Joe's two minutes late. He must have been held up by the opposition."

"What opposition?"

"His mother." Suddenly Alfie tensed. "Look out!" he hissed.

Mr. Detreich was staring in our direction.

Feeling like a fool, I tried to hide my head behind a yew branch.

"Don't move," Alfie ordered.

After a couple of seconds he announced in mechanical tones, "Friendly forces approaching to be identified on far perimeter. Forces wearing jeans, plaid shirt. Yellow hair, shoelace untied on left sneaker."

Joe was bellying along the side of the Detreich house. I could see his plaid shirt and jeans, but I couldn't tell if his left shoelace was untied. Like Alfie, he clutched the tube from a roll of paper towels in one hand.

Alfie cupped his free hand around his mouth and spoke as if into a transmitter. "A2 to J1. Enemy forces approaching from the right."

"J1 to A2," Joe responded loudly.

Mr. Detreich jumped and almost dropped the garden hose.

Pink blossoms trembled as Joe wiggled into an azalea bush. "Enemy forces noted and rendered inoperable," he informed Alfie.

"A2 to J1," began Alfie, but at that moment Mr. Detreich aimed a stream of water directly into the bush where Joe was hiding.

A scream emerged from the azalea, followed by a great shaking of leaves and flowers as Joe erupted from the bush. He crossed the lawn and charged across the street.

Lucky for Joe, there weren't any cars coming.

He arrived safe on our side of the street, his cardboard tube still clutched in one hand.

Mr. Detreich continued watering his azaleas as if nothing had happened. Mittsey began washing her chest.

I crawled out from under the yew, followed by Alfie.

"This mission was a disaster," said Alfie, eyeing Joe with disgust.

"I didn't know Mr. Detreich was armed."

"You could have looked!" Alfie sighed dramatically, then asked, "You want to go over to Sammy's?"

"I have to take Frank's tape of torture sounds home first," said Joe. "Julius wants to borrow it."

When Alfie went into the house to get the tape, I asked Joe, "Why does your brother hang around with Julius anyway?"

"He likes him."

"Do you?"

"I don't know." Joe pulled his wet shirt away from his stomach. "Julius is the only other boy on our street the same age as him. That's how they started out as friends when they were little."

"But Peach Fuzz—" I began, then stopped. Trying to sound casual, I asked, "What is Julius going to do with the torture tape?"

"I don't know."

"You sure don't know much," I said sarcastically. "You're a lousy spy."

"I am not!"

"Are too!"

Joe stuck his face into mine and yelled, "*Am not*!" Then he added in a normal voice, "I've found out lots of stuff."

"Like what?"

"That Julius wants Peach Fuzz to help him wreck the school play."

"*Everybody* knows that."

"And whatever he's planning," Joe went on, "is going to happen in the cafeteria kitchen."

I might have learned more, but that was when Alfie returned. "What are you telling her?" he demanded.

"About Julius wrecking the play."

Alfie rolled his eyes skyward, then shook his head sadly. "You got a lot to learn, Joe," he said. "Never give out information for free. Always sell it."

I didn't want to spend money for information, and besides, I figured Joe had told me most of what he knew. "When Mom gets home," I said to Alfie, "tell her I went to Emily's house."

"A-okay," he agreed.

Emily was sitting on her porch steps, watching Louie, who was in the crate Emily's family was going to use when they took him to Michigan. When he saw me, Louie whined and wagged his whole rear end. He looked like a very small prisoner behind the wires.

"Isn't Louie's crate too big?" I asked.

"It has to be large enough for him when he's grown up. The vet said we should train Louie to sleep inside it and to stay there when we're not home."

"Good luck," I said as I sat beside her.

Emily had changed out of the jeans she'd worn to school into a pair of pink shorts with a matching top. A pink sweat band circled her forehead and put a dent in her fuzzy blond hair. "What did Mrs. Rudolph want?" she asked.

"To know if Sabrina's having problems with the other girls."

"Did you tell her?" Emily sounded anxious, as if I might blame Sabrina's problems on her.

"Only about Sabrina's put-downs." As I scratched an itchy place on my ankle, the charms on my bracelet made a tinkling sound.

"What did she say then?"

"That sometimes we need friends the most when we aren't being very nice ourselves."

Emily scowled.

"I promised Mrs. Rudolph I'd keep trying to help Sabrina," I told her.

"Terrific," Emily said sarcastically. "I suppose you think the other girls will go along with this wonderful idea."

"That's up to you." I was afraid Emily would get mad like before, yell at me, and say we couldn't be best friends if I hung around with

Sabrina. Instead, she leaned back, rested her elbows on the top step, and stared at the sky.

I put a finger through one of the openings in Louie's crate, but he didn't notice. He was watching Emily, his large eyes anxious. When I said, "Louie," very softly, he whimpered. Then he came to lick my finger.

"By the time I get home from Michigan in August, you and Sabrina will be best friends," said Emily, still staring at the sky. "You won't want me around anymore."

"Oh, Emily. That's impossible."

"You think?" She squinted her eyes against the sun.

"There's no way I'd be best friends with the queen of put-down." How could Emily worry about something that would never happen? "You and I will always be best friends," I told her.

Emily looked at me for a long minute. Then she grinned and jumped to her feet. "Want to take Louie for a walk?"

"Sure," I agreed, still surprised that Emily might be jealous of Sabrina. I'd never thought for a minute that Emily and I could ever be anything *but* best friends.

12

Saturday afternoon, Mom and I went to visit
Sabrina and her stepmother. Mrs. Evans looked
younger than my mother, maybe because of the
way she dressed. She was wearing faded jeans and
a man's blue work shirt knotted at the waist with
the sleeves rolled up. Her long brown hair was in
a ponytail, fastened by a red rubber band. Her
gray eyes sparkled and crinkled at the corners
when she smiled.

"You girls already know each other," she said,
waving a hand to indicate Sabrina, who gave me
a quick smile, then ducked her head, staring at
the threadbare carpet on their living room floor.

"Sabrina can show you the stable," Mrs. Evans
told me, "unless you'd like to come along on a
tour of the house."

"No!" blurted Sabrina, then caught herself and
bit her lower lip.

"I guess it's pretty obvious," continued Mrs.

Evans, ignoring Sabrina's outburst, "that our living room needs a lot of work."

It sure did. The yellowing wallpaper was stained by rust-colored streaks and had come loose from the wall near one of the windows. That window had a long crack, temporarily repaired with tape.

On the far side of the room from us, a tattered old sheet covered the carpet. The sheet was littered with bits of plaster, which had fallen from a hole in the ceiling. A large pipe, painted to match the wallpaper, passed all the way through the hole and down through another hole in the floor.

I was trying to figure out what the pipe was for when Sabrina grabbed me by one hand and practically dragged me from the room. She didn't let go until we were outside.

"Come on. The stable's the best part of the place," she said. As we left the grove of trees around the house, she added, "Next week we're buying two more horses so we can give riding lessons this summer."

After the hot sun, the stable was dark and cool. The air smelled of horses and straw, of leather and ointment. I touched the nearest stall. "This looks new."

"It is. My father did a lot of work in here. He even put in a bathroom with two sinks, a shower, and storage cabinets. It's much nicer than the bathroom at the house."

As I followed Sabrina in and out of stalls, the

room where grains were stored, the tack room, and the new bathroom, I wished the horses, stable, and big old house surrounded by trees were mine. "It must be like heaven, living here," I told her as we left the tack room and went back outside. "Do you get to ride every day?"

Sabrina gave a short laugh. "I *have* to ride every day," she said. "The horses need exercise."

"Can't they exercise themselves?"

"Yes, but they have to be ridden or they go wild."

As we crossed the hard-packed earth to the pasture gate, I suddenly realized where we were. "This is the old abandoned farm!"

When Sabrina gave me a sharp look, I thought she was going to say something nasty, but she didn't. Instead, she rested her arms on the top rail of the gate and looked down across the pasture.

I stood beside her, my eyes following the drop of the land to the pond where the muskrat lived and yellow irises grew. I scanned the rise on the other side of the water to locate the apple tree where Emily and I always ate our picnic lunches. "This property runs along the bike path," I told Sabrina. "I didn't recognize it at first because we're facing the Iron Horse instead of looking away from it."

"Iron Horse?"

"There on the other side of the apple tree." I pointed. "It used to be a railroad in the old days, but the tracks were taken out years ago, and the path turned into a bike trail. The trail comes out in town near our school. Emily and I ride our bicycles out this way all the time."

"Can you ride out to visit me?" asked Sabrina.

"Sure. And you can ride to my house."

Near the pond, an old black horse lifted its head, then began to walk up the hill toward us. A chestnut with white stockings followed. Beyond them, on the bank of the pond, a white horse with a big patch of black on its back shook its head, then continued to graze.

"I bet you love this place," I said.

"I like the horses and the stable." Sabrina wiped the sleeve of her orange shirt across her forehead, brushing back a stray black curl. "But I'd like to live in a regular house like everybody else."

"You live in a regular house."

Sabrina straightened, rested the palms of her hands on the rail, and stared at me in amazement. "You have to be kidding!"

"I'm not."

"Since when does a regular house have a sewer pipe running through the living room?"

"That's a sewer pipe?" My voice sounded shocked, even to me.

"You think the pipe's ugly, you should see the bathroom." Sabrina curled her upper lip. "When you sit on the toilet, you can look right down that hole into the living room. Uck. I'd live in the stable if they'd let me."

A vision of a bed set up in a horse stall swam through my mind. It looked pretty desirable.

"It'll take forever for the house to look decent since Jake and Justine are doing the repairs themselves . . . except for the furnace," added Sabrina. "We hired a repairman to fix that. He's already tested the heat ducts to make sure no animals built nests in them."

"How'd he test them?"

"Put off a smoke bomb in the furnace. Smoke poured out all the ducts except the one in the living room."

"What came out of it?"

"A big old momma raccoon with three babies."

"Wow!"

"I wanted to keep one of the babies for a pet, but Jake wouldn't let me."

While we'd been talking, the black horse and the chestnut had reached the top of the hill. I'd planned to stroke the chestnut's velvety nose, but the closer the horse came, the bigger it looked. I shoved my hands into my back jeans pockets.

Sabrina took her hands from the gate to pat at her pockets. As she did this, the black horse swung its head over the top rail. Gray hairs frosted the black face. A small triangle of skin was torn out of the edge of one ear.

Sabrina found a piece of lint-covered carrot in her jeans pocket. She held the carrot on her outstretched palm.

The black horse picked the carrot up with its

lips, then moved away from the fence, munching. When the chestnut took its place, Sabrina muttered, "Oh, no." She rapidly searched her pockets, but only came up with a couple of bedraggled tissues.

The chestnut dipped his head over the gate, snorting through widened nostrils.

Sabrina backed, but she wasn't fast enough. The horse nudged her hard in the stomach with his huge head.

There was an explosion of arms and legs, merging with a blur of orange shirt and jeans. One second Sabrina was standing beside me. The next she was lying on her back on the ground, her legs sprawled at awkward angles. Her mouth hung open, gulping air.

"What—" Something large and powerful struck me square in the stomach. I flipped backward to land beside Sabrina. My right leg dangled through the fence, the left lay across Sabrina's feet. For several terrible seconds the world spun and I thought I'd never breathe again.

Sabrina gave a low chuckle. Then, as she caught her breath, she burst into gales of laughter.

When I pictured the two of us, sprawled side by side in the dirt, I laughed, too. I couldn't help it.

The horse must not have thought we were very funny. He snorted in disapproval, then tossed his head and whinnied. He moved away from the fence, flicking his tail from one chestnut flank to the other.

"He always does that if he doesn't get a treat," explained Sabrina, "and I always forget and give my last treat to Lady."

"What's his name?"

"Red. He used to be a racehorse, but he got sick. Jake bought him cheap and nursed him back to health."

At the sound of his name, Red had swung his head toward us, his ears pricked forward. His eyes were dark and intelligent. A small scar marred the smooth hide at the base of one ear.

I rolled onto my right side and propped my chin on the palm of my hand. I looked at Sabrina, who was brushing dirt and bits of grass from her shirt. "You're fun when the two of us are alone," I told her. "I don't understand why you're so prickly at school."

Sabrina hesitated, then continued brushing at her shirt. Her black hair swept forward over her cheeks, hiding her face from me.

"We want to be friends," I said, "but you act like you're too good for us."

"Too *good* for you?" Sabrina jerked her head around to look at me. "You kids have everything!"

Before I could say anything, Sabrina rushed on. "Emily goes to Michigan for the entire summer," she said. "Marietta was talking about her father's video camera, and we don't even own a VCR!"

"But—"

"Your parents gave you a new ten-speed, and you have a bedroom like a picture in a magazine," she said. "Margo doesn't even know how much her modeling lessons cost."

"We . . ." I said, and stopped.

"I wish you knew what it's like to be poor." Sabrina turned her head, but not before I saw tears in her eyes.

"You aren't poor," I told her. "You have horses and all this land instead of a little bitty lot in town."

"I sure don't feel rich," said Sabrina.

"Neither do I. My family can't go on expensive vacations. Most summers we stay home. And our school doesn't have air conditioning, either, like your school in Florida, or a separate auditorium."

"I only went to school in Florida three months. Before that we lived in Texas."

"This is your third school for fifth grade?"

Sabrina's postcard collection flashed through my mind. I was going to ask if she had cards from every place she'd lived when she said, "With any luck I'll finish here. Justine's grandfather left her this farm, so we own it. I'll probably graduate from high school in this town."

"In that case you'd better make friends."

"Fat chance. The other girls hate me."

"That's because of your put-downs." I touched the charms on my bracelet, making them tinkle, thinking of Emily.

Sabrina pulled a shriveled brown leaf from the cuff of her jeans. As she twirled it between two fingers, she said, "Justine says a sharp tongue cuts two ways, that mine hurts me worse than the other person."

"Justine's right."

Sabrina looked from the leaf to me. "The problem is I can't seem to stop. I get mad and my mouth goes before my brain can stop it."

I struck at a mosquito that was trying to land on my knee. The movement made the charms of my bracelet dash against each other, jangling sharply.

That gave me an idea. "Maybe I can help," I said.

"How?"

I held up my arm, shaking it, rattling the charms. "It's easy," I told her. "Whenever you hear this noise, stop to think. Think *before* you speak."

When Sabrina began to answer, I shook the charms loudly. She stopped, smiled, and said, "Okay. I hope it works."

"It will," I promised her. I'd make it work. I had to.

13

Emily wasn't exactly thrilled by my plan to help Sabrina. "If I knew a way to become popular," she told me Sunday afternoon, "I wouldn't waste it on Sabrina. I'd use it myself."

"You already are popular," I pointed out.

"This is the first I've heard of it."

"I'm not trying to make Sabrina popular," I said. "I only want to help her fit in. You don't have to like her; just pretend not to notice her put-downs."

"That's like pretending not to notice my mother put liver on my plate and gave everybody else pizza."

"When you hear the charms on my bracelet," I said, "make a special effort to be nice."

Emily's lips set in a stubborn line.

"Please, Emily," I begged. "Pretty please."

"All right," Emily finally agreed, "but Sabrina'd better be nice to me, too."

"She will," I promised with more confidence

than I felt. Jangling my charm bracelet might help, but it wasn't going to solve all Sabrina's problems with the other girls. She needed a miracle, and I had no idea how to come up with one.

"Before we begin social studies," Mrs. Rudolph said the next morning, "I want to talk to you about our play.

"We have a lot of great talent on stage," she told us, "but I wish *everyone* in class would take a part. We can use more people for immigrants." She smiled at Sabrina. "Do you think you could help us out?"

Sabrina shifted uneasily in her seat. Then she shook her head.

"Are you certain?" asked Mrs. Rudolph.

"Yes."

"Jason?" said Mrs. Rudolph.

Jason agreed to be the Italian immigrant. Now everyone in Room 12 was in the play except for Sabrina and Julius.

Mrs. Rudolph turned to him next. "Julius?" She asked gently.

"No way!" shouted Rob before Julius had a chance to answer. "I'm not going to be in no play with Julius!"

"Robert," said Mrs. Rudolph.

"He'll make us look like fools!"

"Mr. Ray." Mrs. Rudolph's voice was low, cold, and deadly. "Go stand in the hall."

After Rob went into the hall, Mrs. Rudolph said,

very quietly, "I want all of you to understand that the behavior you've just witnessed is entirely unacceptable, and I won't have it in my classroom." She dropped a hand lightly onto Julius's shoulder. "We'd love to have you join us in the play, Julius," she told him.

"No," Julius said in a low whisper.

"If you change your mind, come to the gym after dismissal." Mrs. Rudolph waited a second, and added, "I hope we'll see you there." Then she left the room.

The door closed softly behind her.

"I don't want to be in the stupid old play anyway," Julius said. His shoulders were hunched together. As he stared down at his desk top, he looked very small.

"Hey, man," said Peach Fuzz. "We can have fun."

"Come on," I urged, but the words barely escaped my mouth. I glanced at Emily, who gave no sign of hearing me. Ahead of me, Sabrina seemed frozen in place at her desk.

The silence in our room stretched longer and longer. I wanted to say something nice such as, "I like you, Julius," but I was afraid the other kids would make fun of me later. Besides, although I sometimes feel guilty about it, I don't like Julius. He's always causing trouble.

At lunch that day everyone was on good behavior. We were so polite to each other I could have left my bracelet at home and it wouldn't have made a bit of difference. Everything was "please" and "thank you" from the students in Mrs. Rudolph's room.

Recess was a different matter. Mrs. Rudolph assigned Sabrina and me to walk together, the last students in line, the last two girls to reach the oak tree.

"If it isn't Little Bo Peep," said Emily as we joined the other girls. "I think your sheep wandered to the other side of the playground, near the track."

Emily, I thought, don't *be* that way! I jangled the friendship bracelet loudly, my eyes on Sabrina.

"If it isn't—" When Sabrina heard the charms, she halted in mid-sentence. "Hi, Emily," she said. "How's Louie?"

Emily must have thought the jangling of the charms was for her. "Fine," she said, not even sounding sulky.

"Did your mother finish making your costume?" I asked her.

"She finished the skirt, but she's having a lot of trouble with the top."

"My mother was going to take me to a costume rental store in Cleveland," said Margo, "but since I'm the Statue of Liberty, she can make my costume out of a sheet."

Although Sabrina didn't look as if she were thinking up a put-down, I rattled the charms just in case.

"Ms. Page gave me a special private lesson on

poise Saturday," Margo added. "She has one opening left in her summer class if any of you guys wants to sign up."

"We're leaving the day after school gets out," said Emily.

"I'll have to sit for my little brother," I told Margo, "so I can't."

Marietta made some excuse; I don't remember what. Then Sabrina said, "I want to take that class, but we can't afford it. Besides, I have to pull my share of the load at the stable this summer."

"What kind of load?" asked Marietta.

"Manure mostly." Sabrina wrinkled her nose as if she smelled something bad.

When Marietta laughed and the other girls smiled, I relaxed a little bit but still kept alert.

"Jake does most of the mucking out," Sabrina added, "but I have to exercise and groom. Since we're getting more horses, that'll be a lot of work."

I was trying to decide if that sounded like bragging when Sabrina's eyes met mine, then focused beyond me, over my shoulder. When Emily, Margo, and Marietta looked, too, I turned to see what they were watching.

Julius and Peach Fuzz were on the far side of the basketball court, too far for us to hear their words, but it was clear that they were arguing. Julius was talking right into Peach Fuzz's face. Peach Fuzz wasn't saying much, but he looked very unhappy. His hands were jammed into the pockets of his brown pants. His orange and brown football jersey was stretched across his round stomach, and the sailor hat he'd gotten for the play was perched so far back on his head it looked in danger of falling off.

"Julius had better be careful," said Margo. "If Peach Fuzz gets mad at him, he won't have *any* friends left."

"He'll have Mrs. Rudolph," said Emily.

"That's good," said Marietta, "because I figure Julius is going to spend another year in the fifth grade."

"Even Mrs. Rudolph won't like him if he wrecks the play," I pointed out. "I heard that's what he's planning, but I don't know how."

Erin's ball went *smack, smack, sprong, swish.* Seeing the five of us turned in her direction, she must have thought we were watching her. After her next basket, she caught the ball before it hit the ground and spun it on one finger.

"Justine told me I could have a picnic on Memorial Day," said Sabrina, lisping as she spoke and keeping her eyes fixed on the ground. "She said I could invite all my friends."

Emily made a sound in her throat, as if she was strangling on laughter.

I threw a coughing fit. I coughed and gasped, bending over double and covering my mouth. Each time I coughed I jangled the bracelet as loudly as I could.

At last, when I couldn't cough any longer, I straightened and wiped tears from my eyes.

"Are you all right?" asked Marietta.

I nodded, one hand at my throat. "I guess so," I gasped, giving a performance Alfie would have been proud of.

On the other side of the basketball court, the argument between Julius and Peach Fuzz had peaked. As I struggled to regain my breath, Peach Fuzz turned his back on Julius and marched across the court in our direction.

Julius ran after him, dodging when Erin's ball bounced off the rim of the hoop. On our side of the court, Julius grabbed Peach Fuzz by one arm and swung him around so they faced each other.

"Let go!" Peach Fuzz tried to jerk away.

Julius tightened his grasp. He made a fist of his free hand, brought it up, and shook it at Peach Fuzz. "You'd better not rat on me!" he said. "It's your tape. I'll say it was *your* idea!"

Just then Julius noticed a parent patrol heading toward them. He dropped his fist, but kept a grip on Peach Fuzz's arm. "You keep your mouth shut," he warned, "or you'll be sorry!"

That was when I figured out what Julius's plan to wreck the play was. The plan wouldn't cause any real damage, because it was only a stupid practical joke. Just the same, it was the miracle I needed for Sabrina.

As the other girls lined up to go inside from

recess, I managed a few seconds alone with her. "Guess who's going to be a hero, save the play, and have everybody turn up at her house on Memorial Day?" I said.

"Who?"

"You!" I laughed at the puzzled expression on Sabrina's face. "I know what Julius is going to do. He's planning to play a tape of torture noises in the cafeteria kitchen. But *you're* going to stop him."

I'd expected Sabrina to jump at the chance for instant popularity, but she didn't. It took a lot of talking on the way into the building and a twenty-minute phone call that evening to convince her to see things my way. I needed all my powers of persuasion to pry an "All right, I'll do it" out of her.

"Believe me, you won't regret this," I told her.

"I hope not."

"Don't be silly," I said. "Julius is only going to play a practical joke. There's no way anyone can possibly get hurt."

I would have been right, too—if I hadn't been wrong.

14

The day of dress rehearsal Sabrina brought picnic invitations to school with her. During lunch she gave one to every girl in Room 12. The invitations were handmade with a drawing of a horse on the front of each one. Inside was lettered:

Hot Dog Roast and Horse Rides
at
Evans Ranch
12:00 Noon
Memorial Day
RSVP 826-2189 by Sunday

From the expressions on the other girls' faces, I figured my plan for Sabrina to save the school play had better work. Otherwise, Mrs. Evans was going to be stuck with a lot of leftover hot dogs.

Recess was canceled that afternoon because of a thunderstorm, and dress rehearsal was horrible. Mrs. Rudolph had to stop it four times to make the immigrants shut up. Peach Fuzz forgot his lines, I had hiccups in the middle of my poem, and Margo collapsed in a fit of giggles. Margo also tripped over her robe on the way off the stage and fell flat on her face.

Sabrina watched from the gym floor, where she sat, legs crossed and elbows on her knees, waiting to go home with me. Her parents were at a horse auction and wouldn't be back until late. Although Mom had invited Sabrina to stay overnight, the Evanses planned to pick her up on their way home.

"That play would make a great comedy," she told Emily and me when we joined her after rehearsal.

"Thanks," said Emily.

"I'm serious. It's better than what's on television."

After the heat and confusion in the gym, the outside air smelled fresh and clean. Already the puddles were drying in the sun. Big patches of blue broke the clouds overhead.

"I wish you could come with us," I told Emily when we reached her street.

"Me, too. I *hate* physical examinations! I don't see why I have to have one every single year before we go away."

"Good luck," I called after her as Sabrina and I headed on toward my house.

Dad was out of town and Mom had to work late that afternoon, so I was in charge of my brother.

"Alfie," I called as we entered the house. "Alfie!

"He's supposed to stay home until he checks in with me," I explained to Sabrina.

"What will you do now?"

"Wait." I looked gloomily at her. "You can be glad you don't have a little brother."

"I do." Sabrina clapped her hand over her mouth to hold back the words.

"Where is he?"

Sabrina didn't answer. She stared out the window over the kitchen table, her back toward me, her shoulders stiff beneath her plaid shirt.

"So don't tell me," I said. "It's none of my business anyway. You want milk or ginger ale?"

"Ginger ale." Sabrina turned, her eyes darting at me, then away again.

I opened the refrigerator door. Maybe Alfie had been home. The bottle of ginger ale had vanished.

"Emily was right when she said my mother didn't die, that she ran away from home," said Sabrina. "She took my baby brother with her, but she didn't take me."

I let the refrigerator door swing shut.

"She sends me postcards, tons of them. The first year I got two or three a week." Sabrina's *s*'s whistled. She stopped to catch her breath.

I glanced at her, then away, at the hen and rooster on the table.

"Last year I only got two."

I wet my lips, feeling sad and a little bit ashamed.

"If you tell the other girls," said Sabrina, her voice almost normal, "I'll say you're lying."

"I won't tell anybody," I promised.

That was when I heard scrabbling at the back door. I ran to open it.

"Alfie!"

Alfie didn't answer. He couldn't. He staggered past me into the house and to the kitchen, where he collapsed onto a chair.

"What's wrong with him?" Sabrina wanted to know.

"Asthma." A great lump of ice seemed to form inside me, raising goose bumps on my arms.

Alfie looked terrible. His face was swollen and an ugly shade of red. All his bright hair was wet, so wet it was matted to his scalp. Sweat poured down his face to drip from his chin.

"Unh-hooh, unh-hooh," gasped Alfie, like before, only this time the sound began deep in his chest, so deep it seemed to come from his stomach. It struggled up through his windpipe and came out his mouth. Then came a horrible retching noise before Alfie began the struggle to drag air into his lungs.

"Did you take your Brethine?" I asked in a whisper.

Alfie didn't answer. He sat on the front edge of the chair, his shoulders hunched forward, his hands on his knees. His eyes glazed as he concentrated his whole mind and body on forcing air in and out of his lungs.

"Did you take your Brethine?" I said more loudly.

Alfie shook his head slowly, back and forth.

"Your Alupent?" I yelled, heard myself, and made my voice calm. "Alfie, listen to me. Did you take your Alupent?"

He nodded.

When I went to the sink for water, my hands were shaking. I had to hold the glass in both of them to take it to Alfie.

"Drink," I said.

"Unh-hooh, unh-hooh," went Alfie. "Unh-hooh, unh-hooh."

The sound was ugly, but worse was the fear that it might stop, that Alfie might not be able to breathe at all. Putting the glass on the table, I ran for the container of Brethine, shook out a pill, and took it to Alfie. "Take this," I told him.

Alfie only continued to stare straight ahead, his shoulders hunched, his face red and covered with sweat.

It was then I noticed white patches on his cheeks and arms. I ran my fingers over one of them. The patches were raised and hard: hives.

"You *have* to take the pill. *Please,*" I begged. "I'll give you the five dollars I have left from my birthday if you take it."

As Alfie reached for the glass, I saw his fingers were swollen, too. That was when I realized his medicine wasn't going to stop the attack. "He needs a doctor," I told Sabrina.

"Why don't you call your mother?"

"It would take too long for her to drive home."

"I'll get a neighbor to take us to the hospital," said Sabrina. "Meet us in front of the house."

When she'd left, I knelt in front of Alfie. I put both my hands over one of his and said, "Look at me, Alfie. Look at me!"

Alfie brought his eyes from their deep concentration to focus on my face.

"Sabrina is getting someone to take you to the hospital. In a little while you'll be better." I swallowed. "We're supposed to meet them out front. Can you walk?"

Slowly, Alfie stood. He managed to walk through the house and out onto the front porch without any help from me, which was lucky. As soon as Sabrina'd left us alone, the muscles in my legs seemed to turn to marshmallow. My head felt as if it were suspended in the air above my body, like a balloon.

The house closest to ours has been vacant for months. Evidently there was no one home on the other side, either, because when Alfie and I reached the porch, Sabrina was headed across the street to the Detreichs'.

The only sign of life at the Detreichs' was Mittsey, who stared out the living room window at Sabrina. Sabrina ran down their front steps and the sidewalk to the street. Although there was a car coming, she ran right into the street and stood there, one hand raised to stop it.

At the last possible moment, the driver put on the brakes. Tires screeching, the car slid toward Sabrina. She didn't drop her hand till it came to a stop.

The kid who was driving leaned out his window. "Hey, stupid!" he yelled. "You want to get blood all over my fenders?" The arm he'd exposed as he leaned out the window had a blue tattoo of a snake. His car was a darker shade of blue, polished to a high shine.

"This is an emergency," Sabrina told him. "A little boy has to go to the hospital."

"So call an ambulance."

Sabrina motioned for me to bring Alfie. As we went down the sidewalk, the kid eyed Alfie, then leaned across the seat to push open the door on the passenger side. I led Alfie around the car and shoved him inside. Sabrina wedged herself in next to me.

What happened next was almost as scary as Alfie's asthma attack. The car's engine rumbled and growled, increasingly loud as we raced through the first intersection. The stop sign flashed past to the sound of tires screeching and horns blaring.

The red blur of a stop sign was the last thing I saw the entire ride. I shut my eyes and hung on to Alfie. When the car went into its final sideways slide, I gritted my teeth and waited for the crash. Then I became aware my stomach was returning to its normal position. The motion outside me had ceased.

Sabrina'd already opened the passenger door and was dragging Alfie from the car. "Thanks!" she told the kid.

The kid didn't answer. He was staring into his rearview mirror at the police car pulling to a stop behind him.

before it slowly opened the passenger door and was dragging him from the car. "He was," she told the kid.

The kid quietly moved. Alfie was crouched on his rearview mirror at the boy responding to a horn behind him.

15

"This is an emergency," I told the woman behind the long white counter in the emergency room. "My brother can't breathe."

"Where's your mother?" the woman asked.

"At work." Alfie's hand was sweating in mine, and he was struggling harder than ever for air.

"Your father?"

At that moment a chubby nurse in a white uniform came out of a nearby room. She glanced at us, then came closer.

The woman behind the counter said something else, but I wasn't listening to her. The nurse had placed a hand on Alfie's shoulder. "Who's his doctor?" she asked me.

"Butters."

"Page Dr. Butters," the nurse told the woman behind the counter. "He went up to Pediatrics." Then she asked Alfie, "What's your name?"

Since he was concentrating on breathing, Alfie didn't answer.

"Alfie," I said.

"Come on, Alfie." The nurse kept her hand on Alfie's shoulder, steering him down a hall to a small room. Sabrina and I followed.

While we waited for the doctor, the nurse helped Alfie onto an examining table and took off his shirt. She also asked me Mom's and Dad's names and where they worked. "I'll have the receptionist call them," she told us as she left the little room.

When she returned, Dr. Butters was with her. He crossed to the table, smiled at Alfie, and said, "Hi there, Al." He glanced at me. "What medicine has Al taken?"

"Alupent, but I don't know when. I gave him Brethine right before we came to the hospital."

"You really got into it this time, didn't you, Al?" Dr. Butters leaned over to place his stethoscope on Alfie's chest.

Alfie nodded, the barest ghost of a smile brushing his mouth.

It was then that I noticed something amazing. As the doctor examined him, Alfie began to sound better. His breathing was still horrible to hear, but it wasn't so desperate.

"We'll give Al a shot, watch his reaction, then give him a second shot," Dr. Butters explained to

Sabrina and me. "If you girls want to go down to the waiting room . . ."

"No," I said.

Dr. Butters glanced at the nurse, who moved in my direction.

Without losing a second, I crossed to the table and grabbed one of Alfie's hands.

Sabrina went along, wrapping an arm securely around my waist. "We'll bite," she warned. "We'll kick and scream."

The nurse hesitated.

"All right," Dr. Butters said a bit wearily. "You can stay."

Not long after Alfie's second shot we heard a clatter of heels in the hall. Then Mom burst into the room. She ran to the examining table and put her arms around my brother. "Alfie!" she cried.

Looking embarrassed, Alfie shrugged away.

"You don't seem too bad," Mom observed.

Alfie *was* better. Not great, but better. His face was close to its normal color and the hives were beginning to fade. Although I was standing next to him, his wheezing wasn't nearly so loud as before the shots.

"You should have seen him when they came in." Dr. Butters shook his head. "Besides the pulmonary involvement, there were hives, swelling, the whole lot."

"What were you doing?" Mom demanded. "Running track?"

"No way," said Alfie. "Joe and me were at Sammy Floria's, doing circuits."

"Circuits?"

"Fitness stuff like in the army," said Alfie. "You run a hundred yards, do ten push-ups, run again, then chin yourself. Sammy has—"

"Sammy Floria," Mom interrupted. "Doesn't he live at the end of Beeson?"

"Yeah."

"But that place is in a swamp!" Mom's voice rose. "It's practically a mold farm!"

Alfie assumed his crafty expression. He eyed the nurse and whimpered as if he were afraid of her.

Mom gave Alfie a stern look, then turned to Dr. Butters and said, "Thank you."

"You should thank the girls. They brought him in and were able to tell me what medication he'd taken."

Mom gathered Sabrina and me into a quick hug. "Thanks," she said. "You make a great team."

I don't know how Sabrina felt, but I was filled with a mixture of pride and relief. We had practically saved Alfie's life. He was probably sitting there right now, grateful he had an older sister. I smiled at him.

"You owe me five dollars," said Alfie. "You don't have to pay me until we get home."

16

The next morning, when Emily and I arrived at school, there was no sign of the Evans's old truck. Sabrina'd arrived early, I decided. She'd be waiting at my desk.

Room 12 was filled with students, all talking excitedly about the play, but Sabrina wasn't among them. I sat with my eyes on the door, keeping my fingers crossed, willing Sabrina to appear. When the tardy bell rang, I leaned back in my seat and uncrossed my fingers. She's sick, I told myself, but I suspected she'd let me down.

Sabrina's absence made no difference so far as my miracle was concerned, because Julius didn't show up, either. Sabrina and Julius are two of a kind, I thought sourly. Neither of them is dependable.

The play was even better than last year's scenes from *Charlotte's Web*. The only person to foul up was me. I forgot my lines.

"The wretched refuse of our . . . our . . ." I said.

"Teeming shore," came in a loud whisper from behind the stage curtain.

A couple of kindergartners in the front row giggled.

I stared at the kindergartners.

"Teeming shore!" said a much louder voice, belonging to Mrs. Rudolph.

"Screaming tore," I said.

I didn't want to be an actress anyway. I'd much rather be a nuclear scientist or a hermit.

After I said, "Screaming tore," a group of huddled masses and wretched refuse crossed the stage to gather at the base of the Statue of Liberty. Some of the refuse wore torn clothes and carried their possessions wrapped in patched bundles of cloth. Others had on costumes of their native lands. Including Emily, there were three Dutch girls in white caps, aprons, and wooden shoes. There was a Chinese boy wearing blue pajamas and a straw hat, and a girl in a hula skirt and red top. Rob Ray wore rags. His wrists were chained together.

Beth Anne was very pretty as an Irish lassie, but Marietta was most splendid of all. She was dressed in a black leotard. Over it, a brightly flowered sarong was tied in a knot at her waist, and her hair was covered by a pure white cloth. A row of bracelets and long earrings of gold, silver, and copper gleamed against her brown skin. She balanced a large clay pot on one hip.

By the time Peach Fuzz appeared near the end of the play, Lady Liberty's arm had started to shake. As I watched through a crack in the curtains, her torch wobbled dangerously. Part of me noted the possibility of Lady Liberty crowning the tugboat skipper with her torch while another part was mourning the failure of my miracle.

As Peach Fuzz swaggered across the stage to the statue, I thought, if only Sabrina had come to school and stopped Julius from ruining the play, I'd be the happiest kid in Oakway Elementary. I glanced at the wall separating the gym from the cafeteria kitchen. My miracle was supposed to have taken place behind that wall.

Peach Fuzz stopped at the base of the statue. He took a pipe from between his teeth and proclaimed in a loud squeaky voice, "Aye, many a cargo of humankind I've ferried across the waters of this harbor. Many a—"

"Eeeiie!" came a shriek from the cafeteria kitchen. The shriek was followed by a scuffling sound and a loud "Ow!"

My heart seemed to hesitate for a second, then beat faster to make up the lost time.

Lady Liberty, the tugboat skipper, and the wretched refuse all looked in the direction of the kitchen. So did everyone in the audience. As they stared, a muffled voice demanded, "You and who else?"

Ignoring the remainder of his speech, Peach Fuzz yelled, "Let freedom ring!"

102

At the end of this scene, the stage curtains were to sweep majestically closed to the tune of "America, the Beautiful." The people in the cast were supposed to stand perfectly motionless, their eyes on freedom's light and serious expressions on their faces. Mrs. Rudolph wanted the conclusion of our play to be dignified and inspiring.

Instead, as the curtains rushed shut at tremendous speed, Lady Liberty dropped her torch and jumped from her pedestal. She gathered up her white gown and ran backstage, down the steps, and across the hall to the cafeteria kitchen. I ran after her. Mrs. Rudolph, the school principal, Peach Fuzz, and most of the rest of the cast were right behind me.

When Lady Liberty burst through the kitchen door, Sabrina was sitting in the middle of Julius's back, his right arm held securely in both her hands. The other arm she kept pinned to the floor with her left knee. Near them, a tape recorder sat on a table.

Mrs. Warren, who's in charge of the cafeteria, had just arrived for work. She stood framed in the doorway to the parking lot, staring over the table at Julius and Sabrina. Behind her, the truck that brings our hot and cold packs was parked with its back doors open. A delivery man stood frozen in the act of removing a tray of hot packs from the truck.

"Let go!" screamed Julius, kicking his legs.

When Sabrina dropped his arm and climbed off

103

his back, Julius scrambled to his feet. His face was red and sweaty, and his eyes were furious. He glared at Sabrina, his skinny body shaking with rage.

"What is the meaning of this?" demanded Mrs. Rudolph.

"She—" began Julius, but Sabrina interrupted.

"We were going to tape the play," she said quickly, "but the wrong cassette got into the machine. We—um—had a disagreement about whether to tape over it."

Mrs. Rudolph frowned as if she didn't quite believe her.

Evidently our principal, Mr. Katai, didn't believe Sabrina either. "Are these your students?" he asked Mrs. Rudolph.

"Yeees."

"You and I had better meet with them in my office." Mr. Katai reached for the tape recorder.

"That's mine," Julius protested.

"Don't worry," the principal said. "Nothing's going to happen to it."

Leaving Julius and Sabrina with the principal, Mrs. Rudolph herded the rest of us down the hall to Room 12. "You people may talk, but stay in the room and keep your voices down," she told us. "We should be back before too long."

Mrs. Rudolph is more optimistic than I am. At that moment I was convinced none of them would be back very soon, maybe never.

"Bye, bye, Julius," Rob said cheerfully as the door closed after Mrs. Rudolph. "This finishes his chances for passing—permanently."

"What about Sabrina?" asked Marietta.

Rob sneered. "She'll start crying 'cause she's in trouble," he said in disgusted tones, "and they'll let her off easy since she's a girl."

"Sabrina's no crybaby," said Margo.

"Yeah, Rob," said Emily. "I don't notice you ever standing up to Julius. You always yell for the teacher."

"Hey! What is this?" demanded Rob. "I didn't do anything to wreck the play."

"Sabrina probably saved it," I pointed out, "and yesterday afternoon she saved my little brother's life, too."

"Come on," said Rob. "You expect me to believe that?"

"It's the truth," I said, and then I told the other kids about Alfie's asthma attack and how Sabrina had stopped a car so we could take him to the hospital.

I had just finished when the door opened slowly and Sabrina came into the room. Her face was pale white against her black curls and she had a large dirty mark on one cheek.

"Mr. Katai and Mrs. Rudolph sent me back here," she said quietly. "They want to talk with Julius alone." Her eyes went across the faces of the other students and for a second I thought she was going to ask us to forgive her. Then her expression became challenging. "I know you guys are probably mad because I didn't rat on Julius," she said. "But I figured he gets into enough trouble already."

That was when I realized something Sabrina'd known all along. Someone could be hurt by Julius's practical joke—Julius.

Since nobody was saying anything, Sabrina added, "I guess I didn't do a very good job of saving the play."

"You did a perfect job," I told her.

Sabrina glanced at me, her slow smile beginning to cross her lips. Then she ducked her head and fumbled at the tail of her shirt, trying to stuff it into her jeans. The bottom button was missing and the pocket was torn partway off, most likely in her scuffle with Julius. She looked up at the kids surrounding her and grinned. "I must look awful," she said.

"Don't put yourself down, Sabrina," said Emily. "I think you look terrific!"

17

When Mom dropped Emily and me off at the Evans house on Memorial Day, Margo, Marietta, and Erin were already there. "Take the girls down to the stable, Sabrina," said Mrs. Evans. "Introduce them to the horses while Jake starts the fire."

On the way to the pasture Sabrina told us, "Jake and Justine bought two more horses Saturday. One of them isn't very well broken yet, and the other's due to foal." As we approached the fence, she said, "After you see the horses, we're going to roast hot dogs and marshmallows. Justine made a cake for us and a big casserole of baked beans. Later we can ride." She leaned over the top bar of the gate and whistled.

Lady was already plodding up the hill, but at the whistle Red wasn't far behind. He lifted his feet high in a spirited prance and trotted into the lead.

"Look!" Erin pointed at Red. "That horse has hair the same color as mine."

"Wow!" said Marietta. "What a beauty."

"He looks scary to me," said Margo.

"You can ride Lady," Sabrina offered. "She's a gentle old soul."

When Red dipped his head over the fence, I pulled a carrot from my pocket. I balanced the carrot on my palm, then extended my hand the way Sabrina had when she'd fed Lady.

Velvet lips brushed my skin as the carrot disappeared. I reached to pat the huge head.

Red snorted softly through his nose.

"Cassie can ride Red," said Sabrina, "since they already know each other." When our eyes met, she dropped one lid in a quick wink.

"I know all his tricks." As I stroked Red's silky neck, the horse put his head close to mine.

"If anybody wants to wash before the cookout, use the bathroom in the stable," Sabrina told us. "The one at the house is a mess."

When we girls passed our car on the way to roast hot dogs, Mom was sitting in it talking with Sabrina's stepmother. Mrs. Evans, who'd been bending to look in the car window, straightened as I approached.

"Wait a minute, Cassie," said Mom. "Mrs. Evans wants to talk to you."

"With so many horses, there are going to be too many chores for Sabrina to handle alone this summer," explained Mrs. Evans. "We'll need someone to help." She paused, then added, "We can't afford to pay, but we'd be glad to exchange riding lessons for your labor."

A vision of Red, his chestnut coat gleaming and his white stockings flashing in the sunlight, danced through my mind. I was dreaming. Any minute now and I'd wake up.

"Cassie?" Mom prodded.

For the first time in my life, I stuttered. "I . . . I . . ."

"Would you like that?" asked Mrs. Evans.

"I'd love it," I managed. "Thank you."

"Come on, Cassie," Sabrina called. "We're waiting for you."

As I caught up with them, Emily's eyes moved from me to Sabrina and back again.

Is it possible to have two best friends? I hope so. The three of us could have great times together, come September.

In between is summer. Emily will be going to Michigan. Margo has modeling lessons, and the other girls from Room 12 will be involved with vacations, reunions, and with their own best friends.

As for me—there'll be no endless hours sitting on the porch steps while days of sunshine and freedom waste slowly away. Swimming and hiking, movies and sleepovers, stable chores and horseback riding are waiting. We still have two more weeks of school, but already I'm certain—this summer's *no* bummer.